SUDDENLY
MY BLOOD
CHILLED—

Looking up, I saw the bell of the tower slowly swinging in its crumbling niche. I shrank back fearfully as a cowled figure stepped from around the remnant of wall. There was something so menacing in his attitude, something so repellent, that I turned and ran. Desperately I made for the gate and flung myself against it.

And then I saw them—a horde of threatening, black-robed figures advancing. They were coming for me. . . .

SIGNET Gothics You'll Enjoy Reading

Dark Odyssey

by Florence Stevenson

A SIGNET BOOK
NEW AMERICAN LIBRARY
TIMES MIRROR

SIGNET, SIGNET CLASSICS, MENTOR, PLUME AND MERIDIAN BOOKS
are published by The New American Library, Inc.,
1301 Avenue of the Americas, New York, New York 10019

FIRST PRINTING, DECEMBER, 1974

1 2 3 4 5 6 7 8 9

PRINTED IN THE UNITED STATES OF AMERICA

AUTHOR'S NOTE

This story, culled from my diaries and from my memory, is a true one. In the interests of those who play a part in it, I have been compelled to change names, if not places. I should have preferred not to resort to this device—I should like the world to know the whole truth, for then I should feel myself truly absolved of guilt in this unfortunate matter. Yet possibly I should still suffer for my sins of pride and obstinacy. I do not know. I know only that I had to set down this account for my own peace of mind. As far as is humanly possible, I have tried to tell the whole truth —sparing nothing, not even myself.

Part One

All my life, I had been told about my Cousin Henry, who had unaccountably left the Yankee fastness of Massachusetts—more specifically, my own native Concord—for the golden shores of California. I had always been eager to meet him, and since I am romantically inclined, I had invented various situations in which I would encounter him —all of these occurring in California, which I longed to visit quite as much as I wanted to see Henry. As it happens, our initial meeting took place in Concord—across my father's grave.

I had no real impression of him in that first brief glance; he was only a tall stranger, whom my Aunt Lucretia identified in the broken whisper that half-served as greeting, too. I, with my eyes on the casket they had just lowered into the earth, did not even realize it when he came to stand beside me. I was too busy with my own thoughts. These were not of the dead, but of those wild extraneous things that come to you when you do not want to concentrate on the immediate present. I was wondering why they always had graveyards on high hills and why the sun was so bright when it had been such a cool, misty morning. I should have preferred the shrouding mists. I could not appreciate the sun and that was selfish of me, for he who lay in the coffin had always loved it. With a sigh, I raised my eyes from the oblong cavity in the grass. That was a mistake, because then I saw Mary and remembered that he would never lie beside my mother. Incredibly, Mary had managed to have my father interred in her family plot so that she might ultimately possess him in death as she had possessed him during the last two years of his life, making him turn his face

from me, his only child—*still* his only child. I shouldn't
have gloated over that. It was a small, mean triumph and I
tried to dismiss it from my mind. I was not entirely successful. That is what hate can do. Until two years ago, I had
known nothing about hate. I knew about it now, I assured
myself grimly. I knew it as more than a word. I knew it as
a person named Mary Booth. Mary Booth *Brett*, I had to
amend. Mary Booth Brett, who was all of five years my
senior and yet whom custom compelled me to address as
Mother.

The laugh, harsh and loud, escaped my lips. The thrust
of my hand against my mouth, my clenched teeth, the taste
of blood on my tongue—all that came too late, far too late.
They had heard it; those black-clad mourners had heard me
laugh over the lowered coffin of my dead father. I, who had
been unable to shed a single decorous tear, who had stood
dry-eyed throughout the interminable ceremonies that had
marked his passing, had laughed—and furthermore, might
continue to laugh in spite of all efforts to choke down those
peals of merriment which had no humor in them.

"Ada!" Aunt Lucretia's bony fingers bit into my wrist.
"Control yourself!"

"Cousin Ada, come." Incredibly, my arm was taken and
gently I was propelled down the hill, made to skirt the tall
gray stones and the polished marble monuments. As I allowed Cousin Henry to lead me away, I realized it was the
second inexcusable thing I had done that morning. But hys-
terical laughter and an early departure did not mean I had
little respect for the dead, did it? I could not have more respect for the man whose body lay in the grave on the hill. He
had been my life for seventeen years—no, for almost nineteen years. He might lie in the Booth plot, but with death
the spell was broken—delicate, pretty Mary Booth no longer had the power to hold him. In death, he was mine. At
the moment I realized that, my laughter fled.

Yet, at the memory of my behavior, my cheeks flushed
and I wondered what manner of excuse I could offer to the
man beside me. Embarrassed, I started to turn away, and in
the action, I stumbled. I would have fallen if he had not
steadied me.

"You are faint," he said concernedly. "Here—we'll sit
down." He indicated a small wooden bench, but I shook my

head. "I am not a woman who swoons, at least not very often. I stumbled."

His smile was the first thing I really noticed about his face. It was pleasant, and broad enough to show me how white his teeth were against his deeply tanned skin. It also brought out fans of creases at the edges of his gray eyes. Through force of habit, I had been accustomed to thinking of Cousin Henry as the golden-haired lad of twenty my mother had so often mentioned. His hair was still a ruddy gold, but he had to be, I realized, at least thirty-five. In the midst of this inadvertent scrutiny, he said, "I'm glad you are not a woman who swoons, at least not very often, Cousin Ada. Indeed, I could not have hoped for more."

His remark was provocative enough to move me to ask for an immediate explanation, but before I could even frame the question, he had taken my arm again and led me from the cemetery toward one of several carriages just beyond the gates.

We had scarcely been seated in its spacious and comfortable interior when he turned to me and said, "You'll not be wanting to stay in Concord any longer, will you?"

I did not even hesitate. I said, "No. I want to go far, far away, as far as ever I can get."

He nodded almost complacently, yet still there was a trace of sadness in his voice when he said, "I guessed that, the moment I was presented to your—stepmother." He added commiseratingly, "I was fond of your mother."

"She spoke of you so often," I told him, thinking what an odd conversation we were having—without formalities, even without preamble, as if we had resumed a long-interrupted friendship, which perhaps we had, since I was my mother's daughter.

"Tilda died when you were thirteen, I believe," he said.

"Fourteen—just two days past my fourteenth birthday—in November, 1838."

"November . . ." he mused. "You were born in November. My wife was also born in that month. She's as proud of her birthday as if she'd ordered it herself. November, it seems, is a mystic month." There was an edge of sarcasm to his tone and a slight frown in his eyes.

"I don't know about it's being particularly mystic," I said; "it's cold, though."

"Not in California. It rains often in November, but even the rain is not very cold."

"The snow came early, the year mother died," I said, remembering it all too vividly—standing at the window in my parents' bedroom, watching the snow fall and trying not to look back at the still form on the bed. I shivered. Death had intruded into my thoughts again, and with it, another vivid recollection—this one, all too recent, of my horrid laughter echoing through the silent graveyard.

"I—I do not know what you must think of my outburst," I faltered. "You were kind to take me away from there but . . . and oh, Aunt Lucretia . . ." I stopped speaking. I was not making any sense.

Much to my surprise, he understood, for he said, "Your Aunt Lucretia and the others will be shocked and express themselves accordingly. You will be polite and contrite. The initial incident will slowly dim in the minds of all those present—to be discussed again and again with appropriate expressions of anger only whenever boredom or self-disgust need assuaging with a scapegoat. You will be unconscious of their censure and untouched by their opprobrium." His laughter was bitter. "There, my little Cousin Ada, I have given you a prophecy and I am sure it's as accurate a prognostication as was ever delivered by Señora Mendoza, my wife's-nurse-who-has-the-reputation-of-being-a-seeress." His smile was mocking but I sensed a deep lurking sadness beneath it.

Since I did not know him well enough to either understand or comment on it, I merely said, "I am sure you must be right, Cousin Henry."

"You are sure of nothing, save that I confuse and alarm you."

"I am not alarmed. I am only grateful that I have had the chance to meet you at long last."

"It's my turn to be grateful," he said. "You are much like your mother, you know. In looks, and you also have her ability to accept the unusual without losing your poise."

"I'm afraid I've no more poise to lose," I said regretfully.

"Come, do not castigate yourself for that. Do you imagine I am your dour Aunt Lucretia? Do you think that I should expect you to act the proper young lady after such stress as has been your portion for more days than I dare to think. Years, perhaps. News does not always reach us in

Monterey, so I cannot know whether or not there was a letter to inform me of your father's second marriage. When did it take place?"

"In March—almost two years ago," I said.

"And for those almost two years, you have been wondering why?"

I nodded, remembering the shock of meeting Mary for the first time and learning almost in the same instant that the fair-haired, childish creature leaning on my father's arm was his new wife! After my father's marriage, I had had a series of recurring dreams in which I explained to an unbelieving mother, "But Mama, you can't come home. Papa has a new wife. You see, we thought you were dead." In those painful, painful dreams, I had never any explanation as to why he had married Mary. I had even less understanding of how she had managed to make him so happy.

"Where did he meet her?" my cousin asked. "She's not from Concord, is she?"

"She was born in Concord," I told him, "but her father, Gaius Booth, who was Papa's best friend, was in the diplomatic corps—he'd been in London for the last five years when he died. Papa was named executor of his estate and so he went to England. He came back with Mary."

A fine cambric handkerchief was pressed into my hand. My companion said gently, "Wipe your eyes."

I started to protest that I was not crying but feeling the wetness on my cheeks, I obeyed. "Thank you," I murmured self-consciously.

"You're very young, but very lovely, too. It's a wonder you're not bespoken, Cousin Ada—or are you?"

"No," I said postively, "and I do not want to be."

He raised his eyebrows. "Never?"

"Not until I find someone who pleases me."

"As a discerning young woman you might have difficulties," he said.

"I might," I told him. "The prospect of remaining single does not alarm me. There is much I should like to do."

"What?" he demanded.

"I should like to found a magazine like Margaret Fuller's *Dial*. Eventually, I shall write both novels and essays and I should also like to teach."

If I had expected him to laugh, I was disappointed, for

his eyes gleamed and he said, "That's very interesting. And meanwhile, you are quite alone?"

I experienced a little twinge of grief and wondered why he was in such haste to remind me of the obvious. "Yes, I am quite alone," I said.

"And, as we've already decided, you want to leave Concord. The only question remaining to be answered is when?"

"When?" I echoed, startled.

"Could you be ready in two weeks?"

"I—I could be ready tomorrow, but . . ."

He put his hands over mine and held them in a warm grasp. "The idea occurred to me when I first saw you, Cousin Ada—and our conversation has only strengthened it. One of the reasons I came East was to find a competent teacher. You see, I have two children, both shamefully neglected."

"Neglected?" I said in surprise.

"Oh, not in any maternal sense. But educationally speaking, they are woefully ignorant. They have their letters and their numbers—in Spanish. However, they've not ten words of English between them, surrounded as they are by a host of Spanish cousins and Indian nurses, nor have I had the time to teach them. Consequently, I meant to bring back a governess or a tutor. I'd not made up my mind. It seems to me that you'd be an ideal solution to my problem. Not as a governess, you understand—you'd be our guest—though naturally, I should recompense you for your services and . . ." He paused, and looked at me appealingly. "Perhaps I should not have spoken so soon?"

I said, "You—want me to come to—to California?"

"Does the thought of such a long journey intimidate you?"

"No!" I cried, caught in the grip of an excitement that served to obviate my grief, if only for the instant. "Oh, no, it does not frighten me. I've always wanted to see California, ever since Mama started reading me your letters. They were like fairytales to me, more beautiful than fairytales because they were real—you, your hacienda, your wife, who must be as lovely as any fairy princess. Do you know that I learned Spanish because of your letters?"

His eyes widened. "You speak Spanish?"

"Oh, yes," I said, a trifle complacently, I fear. "I speak it very well—I am thought to be excellent in languages!"

Astonishingly, he flung his arms around me and held me close. "Perfect," he breathed. "Quite, quite perfect. Cousin Ada, you've wrought a small miracle. You have made me believe in fate!"

A half hour after Cousin Henry had deposited me at my home, I sat in my room staring at a page in my diary, wondering if the extraordinary meeting I had just recorded had really taken place. I had seen the death of so many cherished hopes that I could hardly believe in the granting of this, my very dearest wish! Yet substance was lent to shadow by the presence of his crumpled cambric handkerchief with its beautifully embroidered E in the corner. I had still been clutching it when he left me in the hall. I planned to wash and iron it and return it to him.

Examining it, I mused out loud, "E." I frowned. "But his name is Henry."

"Enrico and Henry are one and the same in Spanish, dear." I heard the words as clearly as if they had been spoken. It was Mama who had given me that information; she had told me a very great deal about Cousin Henry, all of which I had set down in my diary.

On an impulse, I went to the little horsehair trunk that contained all I treasured the most—the locket with the ivory miniatures of my grandparents, the string of matched pearls that had belonged to my great, great-grandmother, a small unframed oil of my father, and my diaries—fourteen of them, one for every year since I had learned to write.

They had been started as an impetus for me to improve my penmanship, and the first book was partially devoted to crooked rows of letters. My initial entry, equally crooked and misspelled besides, read: "Miz Farwether lyed about me." Miss Fairweather had been my first governess.

On writing those sentiments, I had found something I really needed in a houseful of adults, a confidant. My diary had all the attributes of a cherished friend, including those which real friends rarely possess; it neither criticized nor contradicted me. Without it, I should have been much more lonely, for I had no brothers or sisters, and while there were friends at school, I could never bring them home to tea nor to play in the garden because my mother was much too ill to bear their noise. Consequently, it became my habit to spend my leisure hours writing all my innermost thoughts in as much detail as I believed they merited. I was also most punctilious about setting down the daily events of my life. I did this in a variety of literary styles, reflecting the authors I was reading at the moment. That is why some pages read like Sir Walter Scott, others like Jane Austen, Mr. Dickens, and most recently Mr. Hawthorne, whose *Twice-Told Tales* had thrilled me—especially since I had a nodding acquaintance with him since he had just moved to Concord.

My diary had served many purposes. During my tempestuous childhood, those years when I had loved and hated with equal abandon, it had helped me maintain a stiff, decorous appearance before the world, while my written sentences seethed with secret rages. It had been my saving grace after Mama died, for I had recorded so many of our conversations that at the flick of a page, I could summon her to my side. It had been equally easy to find the father I had loved before his second marriage had destroyed my faith in him and my illusions about men in general. It is not easy to see what you had believed divinity turn out all too human and subject to such weaknesses as a young girl's kisses, saccharine endearments, and . . . other things I could not even bear to write. Still, it had been a relief to confide some of my troubled thoughts during those unhappy years, and of late, I had traced the progress of his last illness until that painful moment when I had held his hand and silently begged God to take him quickly.

Gathering my books, I went back to my desk and began to leaf through them. I found many entries concerning Cousin Henry, more than I had anticipated or remembered. Indeed, my parents had spoken about him quite often. At the end of two hours, I had compiled a reasonably complete account of Henry Slade, at least as he was known to my family. To stave off by encroaching grief, I determined to write it down in as much detail as I could provide, and for the purposes of my present narrative, I include it.

To understand Henry Slade and even Ada Brett, I suppose it will be necessary to mention that we come of Puritan stock. Our common ancestor was one Jonathan Slade, carpenter, who came to this country in 1624, settling in the Plymouth Colony. In eight generations, the carpenter's descendants became, say, the equivalents of English squires, but they were as proud as earls after such exploits as hanging witches, robbing Indians, flavoring Boston Harbor with English tea, fighting in both the American Revolution and the War of 1812, and producing farmers, soldiers, judges, bankers, doctors, teachers, merchants, and a man whose crimes were so heinous that his name as well as his birthdates were stricken from the family Bible in a smear of black ink.

Henry was the second son of my mother's brother, also Jonathan, the name being handed down from father to son with depressing regularity throughout all those eight generations. He was born in 1808 when Mama was fifteen. Somehow she became especially attached to him, perhaps because her brother and his wife lavished so much love on their firstborn son—Jonathan, naturally. There was a story about little Henry nearly disrupting Mama's wedding with loud inconsolable wails; he had further scandalized the wedding guests by thrusting his minute fist into my father's face. Eventually, he forgave and was forgiven, for entries in my diary mention his visits in the days when I spelled "Cousin" without the "u" and with an "e" instead of an "i."

In 1828, I wrote that Cousin Henry had gone to Boston to work for an importing company and that Mama had weeped and weeped. In 1830, I had another entry concerning his departure for California on firm business. When Mama wept again, I could spell her emotions correctly, and at ten, perhaps I could even understand them, because the idea of Henry remaining indefinitely in Monterey seemed bleak—especially when I was quite as curious as Mama to meet the beautiful (according to his letters) Señorita Pilar Consuela Maria de Villenueva y Moncado. Who would not long to see a being whose skin was white as a magnolia petal, whose hair was ebony black to match her tilted eyes, who rode like a man but who could dance the most intricate steps in the world with a wine glass poised on her head and not spill a single drop of the liquid inside?—though why she should want to perform such a feat was beyond both Mama and myself. I remember that inspired by that particular letter I tried to balance a water glass on my head with extremely wet results. Mama and Papa both hoped Henry would bring his bride back to Concord for a visit, but he never did. Perhaps because of that early neglect, his

ties with his own parents were loose enough to allow him to
marry his señorita and start his family without much more
than an occasional letter. He wrote more often to Mama.
We heard about the birth of his son Javier, a name I much
preferred to Jonathan—especially after I met Cousin Henry's brother, a thin, humorless man who constantly com-
pared his daughters' accomplished samplers to my own in-
ept efforts. Enough of him! Soon after the birth of his
daughter Rosa, Henry was deeded a vast tract of land by
his father-in-law and started building a house—or, as he
termed it, a hacienda—which when finished would be
called the Casa Slade, to my mind a most unpoetic coupling
of Spanish and English. It was constructed of adobe, a ma-
terial composed mainly of mud and as foreign-sounding to
me as the ice-bricks Eskimos used for igloos. Indeed, for
want of a better example, I had envisioned Cousin Henry
and family dwelling in a mud igloo!

I must confess that when I reread this portion of my diary, I glanced nervously at my rose-patterned wall paper, my
marble-topped mantelpiece, and the frilly white curtains of
my three windows. In contrasting my known comforts with
the possible rigors of the primitive West, I shivered slightly,
wondering if I had not been a trifle too eager in acceding to
Cousin Henry's proposal. I also felt actively affectionate toward Concord, with its revolutionary past so eloquently described by Grandfather Brett, who had remembered when
"our intrepid Minute Men" drove the British back to Lex-
ington. I myself had been present when they had unveiled
the granite obelisk inscribed with Mr. Emerson's poem
commemorating the event. Was it only six years ago that
my parents and I had watched those ceremonies? Yes, there
was the entry in my book, and, in my head, the vision of
Papa with frail Mama leaning on his arm while a little
breeze from the river rustled through the ancient elms. The
book slid from my lap, and the tears I had tried to swallow
escaped from behind my eyes and rolled down my cheeks. I
cried for a number of reasons—grief, fear, loneliness, and
beneath or beyond all that, a definite premonition of trouble to come. I might add that I have had these inexplicable
sensations since childhood, when at one time or another I
had dreamed or envisioned an entire segment of the future
—usually something utterly commonplace such as the redec-
oration of the old schoolhouse, but made uncommon by

my having first viewed it with my inner vision. On this occasion I did not see anything, but I felt that in accompanying Cousin Henry to California, I was beginning an—an—odyssey. In searching for an adequate appraisal of my feelings, I had resorted to the classics. I liked the analogy that occurred to me so much that I intoned it aloud: "I am beginning a dark odyssey." I shuddered; my words had an ominous ring. "Ulysses came home safely," I whispered. "Will I?"

"A chaperone!" Incredulously, I repeated Mary Booth's words, staring at her with a mingling of anger and annoyance. "He is my cousin!"

The argument had been long, violent, and certainly not anticipated. When I had outlined my plans to my stepmother, I had expected she would be relieved at such an easy solution to the problem of living with me in my father's house. I had never tried to disguise my feelings about her. I could only guess that while she had never displayed an open aversion for me, she must have felt much the same as myself. I had not expected her to cry proprieties at me—to stand in our darkened parlor and say steadily, "Ada, you cannot make that long journey in the company of a single gentleman. A cousin is not a father, brother, or spouse."

Never had I hated her quite so much! "Are you implying, Madame, that my cousin—a married man—that he—that we—"

"You must think of your reputation, Ada," she said. "'Reputation is an idle and most false imposition; oft got without merit and lost without deserving.'"

If I had not been so angry, I should have laughed in her face. Papa had been fond of Shakespeare, and to please him, Mary was always quoting him. Her constant and often inaccurate references to the Bard suggested that kind of hasty boning recalcitrant scholars are wont to do before final examinations. I said scathingly, "I do not see that your quotation from *Othello* is at all appropriate, Mary."

She flushed. "The latter half is," she defended staunchly, "and whether it is or isn't is not our concern at present. You are not of age and I cannot allow this unseemly flouting of convention."

"You cannot allow it," I repeated. "How does it concern you?"

"As your guardian, it concerns me greatly," she retorted. "My what?" I demanded, incredulously. "Nonsense!"

"It is so written in your father's last will and testament, Ada, as you will discover when Mr. Ames reads it tomorrow afternoon."

I stared at her in horror, "That cannot be true. Papa would not—he didn't—he . . . "

"He did," Mary said. "Knowing you to be of an impulsive nature, he decided you needed mature guidance until you came of age."

"Mature guidance from *you*?" I demanded insolently.

"Yes. Your father trusted me," she said. There was a strange expression in her eyes; it seemed to be compounded of wonder and gratitude. She continued in soft but firm tones: "He knew he could depend on me." Earnestly, she added, "Ada, you must abide by my decisions. I know what's best for you. I truly do."

"You . . . " I choked back my words. To have expressed any of the sentiments welling up in my throat would scarcely have furthered my cause. Striving to be calm, I said, "Oh, well, if I must be chaperoned, whom would you choose?" No sooner had the question left my lips than I had a horrid presentiment. Would she appoint Aunt Lucretia?

She did not. Her choice was so appalling, I could scarcely believe my ears. "I shall go with you, Ada," was what she said.

"You!"

She nodded, seemingly unaware of my reaction. "I know your father would have wanted it." She raised suddenly tear-drenched eyes toward the ceiling, in lieu of the heavens she was obviously indicating, and clasped her hands in one of those prayerful attitudes she loved to assume. Being small and slight, with a translucent skin, big blue eyes, and a wealth of clustering golden curls, she looked deceptively angelic. Her black gown accentuated her ethereal qualities; had Papa been present, he would have called her "my little Botticelli," one of the many endearing phrases with which he was wont to describe her. However, as I yearned to tell her, the effect was quite wasted on me.

"And are you going to ask my cousin to pay your passage as well as mine?" I inquired coldly.

"I shall pay for us both, Ada," Mary answered equably.

"I am sure your papa would not have wanted you beholden to your cousin."

I was not misled by her seeming generosity. It was only one more odious demonstration of her power over me. Mary Booth was finally having her revenge for my determined if unexpressed antagonism of the last two years, and it was my own father who had provided her with her weapons. I felt dreadfully betrayed and angry, yes, even toward Papa. I could not understand how she had forced him to accede to her wishes. He had been aware of my attitude toward Mary. It had been a constant source of friction between us. "Ada," he had often said to me, "you ought to be friends with Mary. She would be so grateful for your companionship and she is really very fond of you."

"Fond!" He might have been deceived by her cloying sweetness, but I never had been. I knew her to be selfish and self-seeking. As Aunt Lucretia had remarked, "What girl of twenty-one allies herself with a man nearly thirty years her senior? Do not tell me she loves him!" My father? Naturally, he had been flattered by her spurious adoration and . . . as usual, I could not begin to understand the reasons behind his hasty, ill-considered marriage. Then I recalled my conversation with my cousin. His estimate of my stepmother had tallied with mine. When Mary thrust herself forward as an unwanted member of our expedition, probably he would find a way to circumvent her wishes. I tried not to sound too complacent when I said to Mary, "You'll need to speak to Cousin Henry concerning these arrangements."

It seemed to me that she looked vaguely alarmed at the prospect, but there was no tremor in her voice as she answered, "Yes, I shall—as soon as possible."

It should prove, I thought, a most interesting and—for sweet Mary—a most enlightening session.

"Woe is me! Mary is a witch!" I wrote in large shaded capitals across an entire page of my diary. As I reread my exclamation, I wished vainly that it were 1692 and that I was an inhabitant of Salem, Massachusetts, where the merciless, bigoted church elders had needed but a single denunciation to set the dread machinery of injustice in motion. Yet, a second later, I avowed hastily that I really did not wish actual harm to Mary, for as Shakespeare put it,

"Bloody instructions being taught, return to plague their inventor."

Gnawing the tip of my pen angrily, I started writing again, reliving as I did the events of the past hour.

I had been in the parlor when Ruth, our maid, had ushered in Cousin Henry. Fortunately, Mary had not yet come down and I could tell him what she intended. From his expression, I discerned that he was as distressed as myself, but before he could comment, Mary joined us, smiling shyly at him. She received no answering smile from him; his own expression was quizzical and a trifle suspicious. His reaction pleased me. Here, I realized, was one man she would not be able to charm.

Yet, after Mary explained her position on the matter, I was appalled to see him nod gravely. "Yes, Mrs. Brett," he said seriously, "you might be right. The young women of Monterey are very strictly chaperoned by their duennas. I am sure the same would be expected for Ada. I'd not considered the impropriety of her traveling with me."

"But . . . " I began.

"Ada, please," Mary said softly. "You do agree with me, Mr. Slade, do you not?"

He nodded again, "An unmarried girl does need a chaperone, Ada," he said firmly, "and if Mrs. Brett is willing to provide that companionship, we must be grateful." He looked at Mary doubtfully. "However, I should tell you—it will be a long voyage, Mrs. Brett, long and tedious. Are you sure you're strong enough to undertake it?"

Inwardly, I breathed a sigh of relief. He had not failed me. He had discovered a way to discourage her. I rushed to his aid. Assuming an expression of deep concern, I said, "My stepmother has, as you can see, a very delicate constitution."

"I have always found a sea voyage strengthening," Mary said.

"But not around the Horn," my cousin said. "You'll encounter heavy weather, Mrs. Brett—even good sailors like myself have been prostrated in storms off Panama."

"I've been in storms at sea," Mary said. "Father and I traveled a great deal. Once we were in a dreadful squall off Morro Castle. We were aboard the *Egret* at the time and her captain told me I was an able seawoman." Her eyes gleamed at the recollection.

To my chagrin, I detected admiration in my cousin's glance. " I know the captain of the *Egret*," he said, "and so I must take you at his word, which is not given lightly. But can you leave Concord so easily?"

She nodded. "With Arthur gone, there's nothing to keep me here. I shall be glad to go."

It occurred to me that Mary was more devious than I had imagined. She wanted to see California and I was her excuse. I tried to convey this information in a speaking glance at my cousin, but could not catch his eye. He was looking at Mary. "It's been difficult for you, these past months, I'm sure," he said, more sympathetically than I liked.

She seemed to droop. "A little," she sighed.

I stiffened. She was making a deliberate attempt to arouse his pity. I hoped he would see the guile behind it and I made yet another effort to engage his attention. Again, I was unsuccessful. He continued to look at Mary! He said, "I think you will like California."

"I'm sure I shall," she agreed.

I had one more arrow to release. "Mary can never be ready in two weeks time," I said sharply.

"Do we have only two weeks?" Mary said, looking distressed.

To my chagrin, Cousin Henry, frowning at me, said, "I had thought to leave in two weeks, ma'am. I've booked passage aboard the *Mary Anne*, which has comfortable accommodations. Still, if you need more time, I shall arrange it."

She paused and then shook her head. "Comfort is of the essence when you spend many months at sea. I will be ready in two weeks."

He kissed her hand. "Thank you, ma'am," he said. "I am glad you are coming with us."

I stared at them desolately. It had happened again. Just as Mary had conquered my father, she had had a similar success with my cousin. I longed to tell them I did not want to go to California, but since no one but myself would have suffered for the lie, I remained silent. He avoided my glance, as he made his farewells—his smiles were all for Mary Booth. I felt betrayed and bereft. In three days time, I had lost both a father and a cousin!

On a morning two weeks later, I arose early and dressed hastily. We were to leave for Boston at ten, and I had suddenly been seized with an odd reluctance to part from my old home and from the town where I had spent most of my eighteen years, excluding only a few summer visits to Maine. Stealing out of the house, I stood for a moment on our wide porch, savoring the delicate chill of the spring dawn. The air felt fresh and clean, and the paling sky, faintly orange at the horizon, formed an effective background for the huge dark elms that fronted our street. It seemed to me that I had never really appreciated their beauty before, those great trees with their hosts of drowsy birds just beginning to stir.

As I let myself out of our gates and started down Monument Street, I planned to climb Nashawtuc Hill so that I might have a last look at the entire city. With a new awareness, I passed each elderly house along my route, looking lovingly at their ivied sides, their green shutters, their spindly iron weathervanes. When I reached the river that circles our town, I gazed upon its still waters with appreciation as well as affection; its current moved so slowly that it seemed more lake than river, and how beautifully it mirrored the emerging sun as well as the bushes and trees that grew along its banks! Yet such was my mood that a second later I was more melancholy than nostalgic, and turning resolutely from my goal, I hurried in another direction. My tryst was no longer with the hill but with my father.

The sun had entirely escaped the restraining clutch of the far horizon by the time I reached the cemetery. I hurried up the slope. The place where they had buried him was as yet undignified by a stone, but there must still be the faded wreathes and bouquets that had graced his coffin at the funeral. Yet when I reached the site I found them gone; only one bouquet remained—a bunch of roses still touched with morning dew and as fresh as if they had just been gathered. A second glance assured me that this was indeed the case and that there was a little card pinned to them. It read: "Goodbye, dearest Arthur, and thank you, thank you. All my love, Mary."

She had been there before me, and somehow that knowledge spoiled even my last farewell to my father. Cordially hating my stepmother, I went slowly back down the hill, wondering, not for the first time, what lay before me in a new world—where I would still be fettered by chains from the old.

Part Two

There being no railroad station at Concord, Mary had hired a private coach to bring us to Boston. A tiresome journey, it had taken us several hours of unremitting jouncing over the indifferent road stretching between us and our destination. However, it would have been worse by stage, and at least we had been spared the discomfort of importuning strangers, the inevitable odor of sweat and onions, and the crowding one encounters in these conveyances.

My mood during most of that ordeal had alternated between exhilaration and annoyance—the one at the prospect of Boston and ultimately California, the other at the presence of Mary, who fortunately proved a very silent companion. She sat as quietly as the motion of the carriage permitted, her face swathed in the black veil she had not troubled to lift, not even inside—a circumstance that did not surprise me. Undoubtedly, she was determined that I, as well as the world, must needs believe her to be in the very depths of despair. In the two weeks that had passed between her decision and our departure, she had been the subject of considerable and often caustic comment from our friends, none of whom thought it fitting that a new-made widow embark upon a journey of some thirteen thousand miles in the company of a personable man. Indeed, I reasoned wryly, there was now a question as to which of us needed the chaperone.

It was late afternoon when we arrived at the American House, where my cousin had reserved us rooms. It was one of the newest, most luxurious hotels in the city, but by the time we had been ushered into our suite, neither of us could appreciate its wonders. Equally sore and weary, we went to bed in our separate chambers.

I awakened toward evening, feeling considerably refreshed. Slipping from my bed, I ran to the window. Though it was close on seven, the sidewalks were filled with more people than I had ever seen in one place. Crowds of men and women were walking in all directions, while the wagons, hackneys, and coaches in the streets seemed in danger of crushing each other as their drivers urged their horses forward, shouting and gesticulating wildly. It was an exciting scene. I longed to be part of all that activity. Impulsively, I opened my trunk, intending to dress hastily and take a stroll, but just as I lifted out my gown, there was a tap at my door.

"Ada," Mary said tentatively, "I hope I didn't awaken you."

"No," I said ungraciously. I had forgotten about Mary.

"Good. You'd best dress for dinner. Your cousin's sent word that he's waiting for us in the lobby."

"Very well," I said sulkily. If Mary had not been with me, I should have asked Cousin Henry to take me on a walk around the city, but Mary, I knew, had been in Boston often enough to find such an excursion tedious.

Feeling ill-used, I arrayed myself in my new dinner gown. Its black folds depressed me even more. I hate to admit it, but despite my grief for my father, I was already tiring of the black garments I was forced to wear. At the risk of seeming frivolous, I have to confess that I really hated black because my hair is dark auburn and needs color to complement it. My eyes, too, are changeable—in some lights green and in others gray—and black has always made them sadly dull. I am not vain, but I know that I am unusually pretty, even beautiful, and since we were to take supper in the dining hall, I should have preferred to look my best rather than my worst. With that in mind, I fear I pinched my cheeks to bring out some color in my normally pale skin. Though I did it several times, I raised more blotch than flush, and to my surprise, it hurt—and for several minutes longer than you might expect.

I came into our sitting room to find Mary dressed and ready. She wore a gown of heavy black satin, one of several she had left over from mourning her own father two years back, there having been little time to have any new garments made. Black, as I have mentioned, became Mary, and with her air of wistful sadness, she resembled an engraving entitled "Sorrow" I had once seen in the pages of *Peterson's Magazine*. I wondered if Mary had not seen it, too.

As I entered, she looked up, startled. "Ada, dear," she exclaimed, "you're quite flushed! I hope you're not feverish!"

I fear that a blush was added to my manufactured flush. I muttered, "No, no, it's the warmth in here. It's really very close. Shouldn't we go down to dinner. I expect Cousin Henry must be impatient, by now."

Her concern persisted. "It was a tiresome journey. Are you sure you're not too fatigued, dear? You could have supper sent to your room."

I stiffened. For some devious purpose of her own, Mary wanted my cousin to herself that evening. Masking my anger, I smiled sweetly. "I assure you, Mary," I said, gliding swiftly to the door and opening it, "I am quite up to the exigencies of dining downstairs."

Without further comment, she followed me into the hall, which though illumined by the gaslight which is a feature of the American House, was still rather dim. As we made our way toward the stairs, Mary came to a sudden halt, crying loudly, "Why—why, who is that?"

Startled, I looked down the corridor, but I could see nothing. Mary continued to stare fixedly into space. "What do you see?" I demanded, feeling chilled.

"I . . . thought . . ." She faltered. "But it must be a —a mirror. Yes, certainly—there's a mirror at the end of the hall."

"A mirror?" I repeated incredulously. "There's no mirror. There's only a window—with the draperies drawn." I pointed. "See?"

She paled. "No mirror and . . . you saw no one." She looked at me beseechingly. "Ada, you're sure there was no one, no . . . woman in black, coming toward us?"

Her panic was alarming me. "Mary," I gasped. "What's the matter?"

For a moment, she was silent, peering into the gloom, then she turned away, abruptly. "My old nurse told me . . ." she began, then she shook her head. "No, I don't believe it," she said firmly. "It was a trick of the gaslight. It casts strange shadows. . . . Come, Ada. Let us be going." She clutched my arm with a trembling hand. My alarm increased. Though usually I distrusted much of what Mary Booth said, I saw that upon this occasion, at least, she was honestly terrified. Taking pity on her trepidation, I said lightly, "Oh, come, Mary, American House is only eight years old. I do not think it can have accumulated many ghosts as yet."

"It wasn't a—a—ghost that I saw. It was . . ." She swallowed convulsively. Then, almost defiantly, she continued. "As I told you, it was the light." With a smile that narrowly escaped being a grimace, she added, "Please, we'll not mention it again, Ada."

I was both curious and repelled. Obviously, she had had some manner of hallucination. It occurred to me that if she were prone to such visions, she would be even less welcome as a traveling companion. Yet, as I recollected, I have never known her to act in such a strange manner before. I could only hope that it had been, as she said, some juxtaposition of light and shadow unperceived by me. I said, prosaically enough, "Let's find the stairs."

I received another shock, but of a different nature, when I met Cousin Henry. He had evidently been in an accident, for his jaw was swollen, one eye was badly bruised, and his arm was in a sling. In answer to our concerned queries, as he said calmly enough, "I fell from my horse earlier today. She slipped on the cobblestones."

Mary regarded him anxiously. "But are you well enough to travel?" she demanded.

His smile was oddly sardonic. "I assure you, my dear Mrs. Brett, nothing could keep me from returning to Monterey." He frowned. "But I wonder if I have not been a little impulsive in asking both of you to accompany me. It's a long journey—we might be at sea anywhere from five to eight months, depending on the winds and weather."

A little lump of fear formed in my throat. Was he having second thoughts? Would I lose my chance to see golden California? "We shouldn't have bad weather in summer, should we?" I asked.

"It won't be summer when we round the Horn. Below the Equator, it will be winter," he answered, a frown still lurking in his eyes. "And no matter what time of year it is, the seas around there are always rough and the winds of tempest strength."

"You've told us we'd have an excellent captain and a fine ship," I reminded him.

Cousin Henry's eyes were fixed on a point beyond me. He said slowly, "Still—there's always danger on the high seas . . ."

"I am not afraid!" I said.

"Nor am I," Mary laughed suddenly. "Nor am I," she said again. Then she added soberly, "Fate cannot be circumvented."

My cousin gave her an odd look. "Perhaps you're right," he said. "Still, it is not too late to change your minds."

I clasped my hands. "Oh, please," I said. "Take us."

"Yes," Mary breathed. "Do."

He sighed. "Very well. I hope neither of you will have cause to regret your decision."

"I shan't," I said decisively. "California. It's such a beautiful name."

Cousin Henry nodded. "It's a beautiful place. It could be a paradise on earth."

"A paradise on earth," Mary repeated. "But these are often protected by angry angels."

He started. "Why do you say that?" he said tensely.

She shivered slightly. "It's something I've discovered about—paradises," she said.

His look was enigmatic. "As long as you're aware of that, you will be—in a sense—protected."

Their conversation confused me. I felt both angry and excluded. I said abruptly, "I'm very hungry. Can't we go into dinner?"

His smile was indulgent. "Poor little Ada," he said. "Of course, we will." He offered me his good arm, but I noticed that his gaze remained on Mary. It quite spoiled my appetite.

Cousin Henry, pleading an understandable headache, left us soon after dinner. Mary and I wandered around the hotel, looking at its beautifully furnished salons. However, she was abstracted, and since I never did enjoy her company, I did not complain when she suggested we retire. I did not go to bed at once, however. Beneath the glow of one of those intriguing gaslights, I opened my diary and wrote a detailed account of the evening. I ended it with the words, "Thus passed our last night among our familiar haunts." Even if Boston were not quite that familiar, the phrase read well— it had, I decided, a certain solemn sonority.

My sleep was filled with dreams of frowning angels, all bearing flaming swords with which they sought to bar me from igloo-shaped mud huts incongruously situated in the midst of a raging ocean. Through the turmoil, I seemed to hear someone crying plaintively, "Ada, help me . . . help me."

At length, I saw Mary, struggling in the moiling sea. Even as I would have stretched out my hand to save her, a great green wave closed over her head. I awakened with tears rolling down my cheeks, which shows how utterly incongruous dreams can be, for surely I should never have wept for Mary, however dire her plight.

Our departure from Boston was so harried and hurried and plagued by misplaced baggage, misdirected coachmen, and other confusions that by the time we were actually aboard the *Mary Anne* and scudding past the venerable Boston Light, any homesickness I might have suffered was replaced by relief that I was at the railing watching the shore recede rather than waving wildly from the dock, which could have happened.

Aside from Mrs. Caleb Hardy and Master James Hardy, our captain's wife and small son, there was only one other passenger—he had come to stand beside us briefly as we watched Boston diminish in the distance. He was a tall, frail Spaniard whom the captain introduced as Don Pedro de Vargas, bound for San Diego.

He had acknowledged the introduction with a frosty smile and a brief nod of the head, after which he had stalked away, disappearing below deck.

"Evidently he prefers his cabin to our company," I said.

"So much for the vaunted Spanish courtesy," Mary added, and laughed.

My cousin frowned. "I probably should have told you that some of our resident Californios aren't overfond of Yankees. They don't trust us. The United States is too close and acquiring territories too rapidly for their peace of mind."

"They seem to have trusted you."

Cousin Henry's face darkened. "Not immediately," he

said. "My acceptance was due to my friendship with my father-in-law, Don Hilario de Villeneuva. I met him when I first came to Monterey. I was very lonely in those days and he opened his home to me. It was unusual for a Californio to be so hospitable to a foreigner, but he took a great fancy to me and I to him. Some other members of his family were not quite so cordial." There was a grim expression in his eyes and he seemed to be looking into a distance that lay far beyond the straining ropes of the sails, the screaming gulls, and the foaming waters.

"I hope that changed when you married," Mary said.

"It did—for the most part. Don Hilario was determined it would and when he spoke, they listened. I wish you might have met him. He was a fine gentleman—well-read, too. That's what really brought us together. He loved books. He said they were the wine of the soul."

"The wine of the soul . . . that sounds like Arthur." Mary's hand strayed to the ebony locket that contained my father's miniature.

The calculated pathos of her expression and her gesture escaped my cousin. Taking her hand, he held it warmly in a moment of silent communion that further enraged me. More curtly than I had intended, I asked, "And what of Don Hilario? Is he dead?"

My cousin winced. Dropping Mary's hand, he moved away from us. "Last year," he said in grating tones; "thrown from his horse, so they said."

"So they said?" Mary questioned. "You don't believe them?"

"He was a centaur in the saddle. It seems hard to imagine that any horse could get the better of him—especially an animal he rode every day."

His dour expression filled me with foreboding. "What do you think happened?"

He was silent a moment. "I don't know," he said finally, "and since I don't know, I shan't hazard any guesses. Don Hilario fell from his horse and broke his neck. That's the story everyone, including my wife, accepts. Accidents do happen—especially on rock-strewn mountain trails."

"Rock-strewn mountain trails." That particular description was almost as unsettling to me as his hint of foul play. I tried to imagine what California might be like, but failed. My only impression was one of a sinister strangeness, and for the first time, my excitement at seeing this vibrant new land was neutralized by fear. When Mary remarked, "There's a cold wind blowing, Ada. Shouldn't we go below?" for once, I was quick to accede.

I had intended keeping a faithful account of my experience on board the *Mary Anne*. Indeed, I had written "Ship's Log" across the page in my diary marked April 12th. Unfortunately, my log was filled with hiatuses. The first of these was caused by a bout of seasickness resulting from the sudden squall that arose our third day out, investing our ship with a species of St. Vitus dance. She had rolled and shuddered upon the waves until I was sure we would be engulfed. When the sickness came upon me, my initial terror was replaced by the fervent hope that the engulfing process might not take too long. Eventually, the pitching and tossing subsided, and I was able to sip broth and gnaw upon a dry biscuit, actions which finally convinced me that starvation was no longer either desirable or inevitable.

"I am reborn," I headed the entry for April 18th, and that, indeed, is how I had felt when I awakened to find that the heaving of the vessel no longer occasioned a corresponding "whomp" in my chest. My subsequent remarks, written some six hours later, were less pleasant, for in an effort to acquaint myself with my new surroundings, I had started to converse with one of the sailors. He had been very informative, telling me that I was standing on the starboard side and that the billowing sail directly over my head was attached to the mizzenmast. He had been joined by another member of the crew, who made haste to explain that we were in the bow of the ship. He had started to escort me to the stern and show me the wheel when Mary suddenly appeared, saying breathlessly, "My dear Ada, come, there's something that needs seeing to in the cabin."

The "something" proved to be me. I received a long, solemn lecture on the evils of addressing any member of the crew. "It will be a long voyage, Ada," she had concluded sternly, "and since there are only the three women on board, I am sure you will not want to tempt the men."

I thought her stipulations ridiculous until the following afternoon, when on walking along the deck, I met the eyes of a sailor, leaning negligently against a mast. He was looking at me steadily and there was a hardness in his stare that unsettled me. Even more unsettling was his slow smile and the way he brought out his tongue and licked his lips. I turned away quickly, but oddly, I still felt the warmth of his eyes on my back. Hastily, I returned to my cabin. Even after I had closed and locked my door, I felt a pulse beating in my throat. After that, I took care to speak only with Mr. Philips, the first mate, whom Mary had defined as "safe."

My conversations with him might have been safe, but they were also singularly unsatisfying. A tall, thin man from Newport, Rhode Island, his bony face was reddened rather than bronzed by the elements; he spoke in a dry chapped voice, and he had pale blue eyes which seemed to have seen everything twice. Nothing surprised him. Fierce squalls, high waves, the eerie phenomenon of St. Elmo's fire darting over the mastheads during an electric storm, left him unmoved; and though his attitude calmed my fears, it also vitiated much of my excitement. Thus, when on May 1st the waterspout whirled out of the deep, rising to a veritable tower of angry green water sewn with foam, terrifying all of us and causing Captain Hardy to change course in order to escape its churning backwash, Mr. Philips said. "I've seen others, higher and considerably more formidable."

I was invested with an absurd sense of partisanship for the despised spout, a sentiment I inadvertently confided to Mary—why I do not know. She looked at me with an odd little smile. "You'd be better off bestowing your concern on something more responsive," she said.

Obviously, she meant herself, and she would probably have enlarged upon her theme had I stayed to listen; but feeling intimidated, I went to my cabin to enter the spout in my diary—not forgetting the defiant addition that it was surely one of the most terrifying examples of its kind!

However, by the time several more weeks had passed, I could agree with the phlegmatic Mr. Philips that it was an uneventful voyage despite our share of scenic wonders, buffeting waves, storms, dolphins, sharks, etc. In spite of the activities of the crew, which included the singing of some colorful sea chanties and an occasional march round the deck to the tune of fife and drum, the very length of time we were afloat tended to erase the definition between days, and it would be with some surprise that I would find I had gone as much as seventy-two hours without writing a single word. I can remember only a few occasions when I was stirred from my growing apathy to do more than record the weather or the advent of some unusual sea creature, such as the whale sighted off the port bow or the convoy of porpoises that accompanied us for several days. However, my entry for June 7th took up several pages. On that particular morning, we were some fifty miles off Cape Blanco, and quantities of flying fish were skimming over the waves. With their delicate, rainbow-hued fins and iridescent bodies, they were a lovely sight. Unfortunately, they were equally if less aesthetically appealing to the seabirds, who regarded them as airborne delicacies to be seized on the wing. While I stood at the rail watching this dramatic spectacle of life and death, an immense gull-shaped bird joined the throng, attacking the flying fish with more will than skill. A cry from one of the men alerted me to its identity. It was an albatross!

An albatross! Who could look upon this bird without remembering *The Ancient Mariner?* I quoted softly:

> At length did cross an Albatross,
>   Through the fog it came;
> As if it had been a Christian soul,
>   We hailed it in God's name.

Truthfully, I was daunted by my first sight of the late Mr. Coleridge's legendary bird. Viewed without accompanying fog, it proved to be bulky, clumsy, and possessed of one of the most improbable voices I had ever heard. It brayed!

"He haw, he haw," it shrieked as it grabbed for fish. It was so ludicrous-looking and sounding that I began to laugh. However, my mirth quickly changed to horror as I heard first one shot and then another and discovered that several sailors were actually trying to bring it down!

> And I had done a hellish thing,
>   And it would work 'em woe:
> For all averred, I had killed the bird
>   That made the breeze to blow.

Forgetting Mary's injunctions and my own fears, I sped to the men who were behaving in this unseemly manner. "Stop, stop, please," I cried. "It's an albatross!"

A tall, muscular man with a shock of light yellow hair and bright blue eyes stared at me with amused surprise. "Shure an' it's an albatross, my pretty colleen, and if I hit it, you'll be havin' yourself a fine new purse!"

As he raised his gun to fire again, I made a futile grab for it. "You mustn't!" I shrieked. "Let it be!"

My protests were greeted with laughter and a few muttered remarks I did not catch, but across the deck, Mary cried, "Ada, what are you doing?"

"Ada, for God's sake!" My cousin strode to me and, seizing my arm, pulled me away. I wrenched myself out of his grasp.

"Stop them," I sobbed. "Don't you see what they're doing? Ohhh!" I shrieked as another shot resounded in my ear and something large and white plummeted through the rigging and with one final strident "Awk!" lay dead at my feet.

I pointed at its blood-stained plumage in horror. "L-look," I gasped.

"I'll have its feet," shouted the Irish sailor, snatching at his trophy.

"It's me what got it, Sean," exclaimed another man, grabbing for the bird.

"The hell it was," growled Sean, and then he looked at me. "Savin' your presence, little lady."

Bursting into tears, I suffered my cousin to lead me away. "Ada," he said gently, when we had rejoined Mary, "sailors always shoot birds. It's a great sport with them."

"It—it wasn't a b-bird," I wailed. "It was an albatross!"

> Water, water, everywhere
>   And all the boards did shrink;
> Water, water, everywhere,
>   Nor any drop to drink.

To my surprise, it was Mary who had quoted the verse. She put a conciliating hand on my arm. "It's only a myth, Ada," she said urgently. "Don't take it so much to heart."

"It's based on fact." I wept.

"Fact?"—my cousin—or Henry as I had been enjoined to call him—inquired derisively. "Nothing of the kind. It's a poetic fancy."

"It'll throw ya for the feet, Sean," I heard a man yell.

"For the feet?" Mary inquired. "Why do they want the feet?"

"They make purses from them," Henry explained. "Maybe I can buy a couple for you and Ada. They should be shooting a few more—we're in the region where they're quite plentiful."

"M-more. . . ." I sobbed. "Oh, d-dear. . . ."

"Poor Ada." Mary looked at my cousin. "She has far too much sensibility."

"Indeed she does," Henry agreed.

"She should . . ." Mary began.

My sorrow was abruptly replaced by anger. Between clenched teeth, I said, "I am not *she*. Though neither of you appears to realize it, I am *me*—and *I* am here. When I am not here, you have my permission to say 'she.' You have it now." With that, I went to my cabin, forgetting the albatross in brooding over my other woes.

As I had feared and anticipated, my stepmother and Henry enjoyed a friendship from which I was excluded. Their attitude toward me was both infuriating and frustrating. They acted as if I were a child—I, Ada Brett, who would be nineteen in less than six months! Mary was not that much older; she was only twenty-three, yet—abetted by Henry—she dared to patronize me.

I could not understand why Henry, who had been so sympathetic at our first meeting, could ignore—well, if he didn't actually ignore me, certainly we never achieved the communion we had had that day at the funeral. No, I decided, I was not being entirely accurate. I did understand what had happened. The barrier that had been raised against me resulted in part from the proprieties implicit in the plain gold band encircling Mary's finger. She had been a wife, a state of being that endowed her with both a freedom and an authority far beyond the years that lay between us. Despite my aversion to marriage, I found myself actively envying Mary, and not for the first time, I wondered what being married meant and why it should change a girl into a woman so quickly. That there was more to it than a mere ceremony, I was positive. At school, there had been many secret giggling conversations when one or another older sister had been bespoken. Wifely duties, my classmates had maintained, consisted of considerable kissing. It was from this procedure that children were produced. I knew that for an indisputable fact, though I reasoned that it must be an unusual sort of kiss since nothing like that occurred when you kissed your father or your other male relations. Of course, kissing had not brought Mary any progeny, for all her constant embracing of my father. I sighed. It was very confusing.

As I huddled on my bunk, a glimpse of the sea beyond the porthole depressed me. There was so much of it, and while it had a certain beauty of its own—in the variations of the waters, in the dawn and at sunset—I had grown weary of gazing at it. There were times when I wondered if I would ever see land again, and more than once I had regretted my decision to leave home. In my mind's eye, I walked down Concord's shady streets, lay in the deep grasses of its meadows, or visited that charming couple, Nathaniel and Sophia Hawthorne. I also envisioned Mr. Emerson's dark intense gaze as he disputed a philosophical question with that strange vague man Mr. Alcott. These people knew me; they listened when I talked, they read the scraps of poetry or prose I wrote, and they complimented me upon my artistic imagination. Why had I been so eager to leave them? Irony of ironies, my precipitate departure had been at least partially prompted by a wish to escape from Mary, and here she was, clinging to me like lichen. Reaching for my diary, I began to write. I fear I seeded my account of the late albatross with several digressions, all having to do with Mary's witchlike propensities. While these observations were more spiteful than speculative, I did have an encounter with her that seemed to imbue them with an unexpected credence.

It started with a storm. Henry and Mary notwithstanding, I like to believe that the squall which unexpectedly arose on the afternoon of June 9th resulted from the destruction of no less than seven albatrosses—albatreese? I am not sure of the plural but of their plurality there was no doubt. I hoped that their spirits were in some way propitiated by the towering waves and the broken mast that caused their murderers so much anxiety and extra work. I was not quite so enthusiastic over the fact that my own window was blown out and the interior of my cabin drenched, for it meant that in lieu of other accommodation, I would have to stay with Mary that evening.

She had already disrobed for the night when I came in. I

was considerably startled by her costume. She was divested of her customary black—the peignoir she wore over her nightdress was pale pink and banded with lace—but what really caught my eye was the long necklace she had twisted around her throat. In the wavering light of the whale-oil lamp, it seemed to be made from congealed honey or, even more improbably, from hardened sunlight.

"Oh, how beautiful!" I exclaimed. "It's amber, isn't it? Did my father give it to you?"

For some reason, she flushed, and her hand flew to the necklace, half-hiding it from me. "I—forgot I was wearing it," she said self-consciously. "It—it's such a habit with me to"—she paused then added—"your father did not give it to me. It was a gift from Gwynneth."

"Gwynneth?" I questioned.

"My old nurse. She was a Cornish woman and very superstitious. She said amber would keep me safe whenever I traveled on water."

"Oh, I seeeeeeee . . ." the vessel had lurched and I pitched forward, clutching wildly at Mary. Accidentally, I caught her necklace. To my horror, it broke, sending a golden stream of beads all over the cabin floor. She uttered a strange, agonized little cry and knelt quickly to retrieve them.

Feeling dreadful, I hastened to help her. "I—I'm sorry," I stuttered. "I didn't do it on purpose. The ship . . ."

"I know you didn't," she assured me earnestly. Yet the look she gave me was curiously disquieting. Her eyes were wide and shadowed, and she added in a lower voice, "The purpose is beyond us . . ."

"Beyond us?" I repeated blankly. "I don't understand."

"It—it's an omen," she whispered. "Another omen."

Something in her demeanor reminded me of her odd behavior in the Boston hotel, and instinctively, I knew she too was remembering that night. I decided to deal with her peculiar terrors as I had before, prosaically. Thrusting all the beads I had managed to find into her hands, I said calmly, "Your necklace can be restrung, Mary."

She shook her head. "It would be useless. The spell is broken."

"The spell? You speak as if your nurse was a witch or something. But you certainly can't believe in witchcraft!"

She did not answer immediately. Instead, she went to her

trunk, and taking out a small black leather pouch, she dropped the beads into it and replaced it before turning to me. "Some people are gifted with extraordinary powers," she said in a low voice. "They use them for good or bad." Almost defensively, she continued, "My nurse Gwynneth was good—I know she was good—and wise and learned."

"Was she with you a long time?" I asked.

"Sixteen years. She was the only mother I really ever had."

"She's dead?"

"Yes," Mary looked away quickly, but not before I had glimpsed the tears glistening on the ends of her long fair lashes.

"You still miss her?" I said, feeling a twinge of pity for her.

"Yes," Mary answered in a low voice. "I still miss her. She made me feel so safe, so protected. When she—died, I lost my way . . . and the . . . darkness came." Suddenly, startlingly, she laughed harshly. "Heavens, listen to me! Talk about flagrant self-pity. Talk about . . ." she half turned from me, saying in partially muffled tones, "Please, pay me no mind, Ada. It's the shadows that have wrought upon me. I hate it when the lamps burn dim. I like a bright room. Come, let's go to bed."

I wanted to question her further, but there was something in her manner that suggested she would not take kindly to my probing. "I suppose we ought," I conceded reluctantly.

Usually, the rocking of the ship brought sleep to me quickly, but on this particular night, I lay awake a long time thinking about Mary. The more I knew her, the less I understood her, and oddly enough, I actually wished we were closer; instinctively, I felt she was as lonely as myself. Yet no sooner had I arrived at this conclusion than I remembered I should not have been so lonely or so isolated had not Mary come between me and the two men who had figured most prominently in my life—my father and my cousin. Furthermore, her references to her nurse had been disquieting. If she had spent sixteen years in the company of a witch, might I not be right in my suspicions? Might she not have charmed my father and my cousin by foul rather than fair means?

"Still waters run deep, Ada," my mother had often re-

marked. And Mary was very quiet—she even slept quietly.
I could not even hear her breathe. Nervously, I took a closer look at her bunk, and at that moment a ray of moonlight
illumined her face. Her cheeks were wet. She had cried herself to sleep!

Perplexed and disturbed, I want back to my own bunk,
and when I finally slept, my dreams were as chaotic as my
thoughts had been. However, all I remembered upon waking was something about golden rain descending from a
black pouch-shaped cloud—a vision which, given the circumstances of the previous night, was hardly remarkable.

I see no reason to say anything more about the month of
June than I have already recounted. There was the sea,
flying fish, whales, occasional sightings of other vessels.
Once we sent out a boat to a French frigate and our men
came back tipsy. There were sudden storms and there were
times when the ocean was smooth as glass. I read all the
books I had brought with me and then, thanks to Mr. Philips, I was brought to the cabin of Mrs. Hardy, the captain's
wife—a lady who kept to herself quite as much as the
Spanish passenger. However, she did have books which she
was willing to lend me in exchange for mine.

I was not enthralled by her choice of literature, which
was improbably divided between insipid romantic novels
and religious tracts. However, thanks to the forgetfulness of
a former passenger, she did possess worn copies of Scott's
Rob Roy and *The Black Dwarf* as well as a *Collected
Works* of James Hogg—such an odd name for a man who
wrote so beguilingly of fairyland. Indeed, there was much
in his poem *Kilmeny* that once might have reminded me of
our destination. At the beginning of the voyage, I, too, had
hoped for

> A land of vision, it would seem . . .
> A still, an everlasting dream.

There was, however, nothing dreamlike about the land
we were beginning to see as we approached the coast of
South America, nor was there much pleasure in the viewing, for from the moment the distant shore appeared, we
were visited by strong gales which attacked us with demonic fury. Their impact upon our ship was such that we dared

not stir outside our cabins but huddled in our berths, bracing ourselves against the watery onslaughts that all but tipped us over. Such objects as were not well-secured flew about the decks and were lost in the churning waters. At one moment, I was very nearly savaged by my own sliding trunk. Thus I missed seeing much of that anticipated scenery, though during a period of reasonable calm, I did obtain a sight of Tierra del Fuego, a barren land punctuated by the fires its natives set to keep them warm during the long winter. Its towering peaks were so high their frozen summits were lost in shrouding clouds. It was a vision both forbidding and promising, since its appearance meant our journey had been more than halved and that soon we should be setting foot on land, for, with an unexpected lilt to his voice, Mr. Philips informed me that we would be stopping in Valparaiso for three days!

Yet between ourselves and our projected haven lay the dangerous passage around Cape Horn. Henry had told us it could take from two days to two months, and as we approached the Cape, those furious winds Mr. Philips termed Westerlies screamed out of the skies and attacked the sails. We fled below, but not before we had glimpsed the huge mass of the Horn rising starkly over the sea. It is impossible to describe its appearance in any detail—I did not see enough of it—but I received an impression of seamed jagged cliffs, jutting rocks, shattered crevices—all deep in snow, all incessantly battered by ferocious, wind-hurled waves.

As we sailed through those tumultuous waters, my terrors increased practically by the minute, and I could only pray that if we were dashed against the rocks, I should be drowned before my body was flung upon that fearsome barrier. Contrary to my morbid expectations, we rounded the Horn in a scant five days, and though the seas were rough as we made our way toward Valparaiso, and the gales strong, they were as halcyon zephyrs after what we had endured.

Despite the icy chill in the air and the stinging spray in our faces, we took to spending considerable time at the railing, scanning the horizon for the outlines of the Chilean port. Even our reclusive Don Pedro joined us in this activity, and thus it was that Henry nearly fell overboard!

Even though I witnessed the incident, I am still not sure of exactly what happened. I only know that during one of the ship's customary lunges, Don Pedro lost his balance and fell against Henry, clutching him in a way that forced my cousin back against the railing. Don Pedro was striving to extricate himself, and that only made matters worse, for in his efforts to stand, he only succeeded in pushing Henry further over the side. Fortunately, Sean, that same Irish sailor who had shot the albatross, managed to avert catastrophe by pulling both men to safety. Don Pedro was most dreadfully shaken. I thought he would never stop apologizing to Henry. I wish I could say that my cousin had been equally courteous, but on the contrary, he was very cold and curt, which I thought rude, considering that it had been an accident.

On July 27th, Mr. Philips told us that Valparaiso was only three hundred miles northeast. To me, that seemed far away, but Henry said we should be there in less than a week! Oh, we were excited! After more than three months afloat, the very notion of shore was heavenly. To stand on firm ground, to walk beyond the circumscribed boundaries of the ship, to have a dinner of fresh vegetables and meat that did not taste like cardboard in a room which would not suddenly tilt, throwing you and your food on the floor—all these commonplace activities took on the aspect of rare treats. Mary and I spent hours readying our wardrobes, shaking wrinkles out of our best woolen gowns, attaching new ribbons to our bonnets, unearthing black silk aprons and sealskin muffs.

We arrived in the harbor in a record four days, on the morning of July 31st. It was a moment that drew cheers from the crew, and again our Spanish passenger, albeit very timorously, joined us at the rail, standing a considerable distance from Henry. We—Mary, Henry, and I—had been there since dawn, but despite my exultation, I could not help being disappointed. It was only one more bleak mass of land, encircled and bisected by high snow-patched hills against which such buildings as we could discern were small and poorly constructed from a mixture of what Henry explained was mud and straw. If distance failed to enchant us, proximity was even less enticing.

We dropped anchor in a harbor filled with small fishing craft. There were also two schooners, one from Norway and another from Gloucester, Massachusetts. Our crew, seemingly maddened by the promise of shore leave, exchanged shouts and signals with such personnel as still remained aboard these, and after the comparative quiet of the high seas, we were nearly deafened by the sounds rising on all sides of us. These increased as the boat that was to take us to shore was lowered. I was chagrined to find that though the air was full of Spanish phrases, I could understand little—for it was spoken rapidly and in a dialect never used by my teachers.

As we were rowed toward shore, it seemed to me that the entire population of Valparaiso was awaiting us—and this despite the chill winds and the dampening drizzle. Hundreds of men and women, shouting, gesticulating, and waving, were assembled on the quay, and as we were helped up crude ladders to the dock, they pressed forward excitedly, fingering our gowns and peering into our faces with an outspoken admiration more frightening than flattering.

Placing himself between us, Henry clutched our arms and, uttering what I took to be a stream of Spanish epithets, attempted to force a passage through the crowds. I helped him by furling my umbrella and using it as a club, and Mary followed suit. Eventually our desperate measures had some small effect—they parted before us, leaving us enough room to walk. Still our progress was slow, impeded by hordes of small boys who seemed to have been sown into the soil like dragon's teeth to spring up magically before us, shivering extravagantly and extending small hands, red with chilblains, for coins. By the time we had gained the muddy road that served as main street, I was feeling faint, for the crowds were daunting not only in their proximity but in their odor. Then, too, there was the dampness of the air, which made our garments seem waterlogged and thus twice as heavy.

I hoped we might go to a hotel, but Henry had another destination in mind. It was, he told us, the home of an old friend, a member of his former firm. It was located halfway up one of those ubiquitous hills, and we reached it by donkey cart. It was an uncomfortable journey, for the roads were dreadful—slick and muddy—but our destination proved a real oasis; it was a large adobe house, built around a courtyard that must have been very pleasant in summer, for there was a fountain in the center and in niches along the walls there were pottery jars filled with assorted greenery. Even more to my liking was the interior of the house, into which we were ushered by a small manservant in curious loose garments of embroidered wool. It was pleasantly warm, and because its small deeply recessed windows let in very little light, candles flickered in sconces on the walls and in wrought-iron fixtures descending from the ceilings.

When my eyes had become accustomed to the dimness, I saw that we were in a spacious room furnished with rough-hewn wooden and leather chairs, a long table flanked by benches, and a most incongrous Chippendale desk. Both the whitewashed walls and the tiled floor were covered with brightly colored woven rugs, and a huge fire was burning on an immense hearth. It was different from anything I had ever seen, but as I sank down on a chair, I felt as if I should never want to rise again.

Mary settled in the chair next to mine. "Oh," she breathed thankfully, and put my thoughts into her words: "I feel as if I could stay here forever!"

"My pleasure!" exclaimed a voice which was appreciative, male, and British in accent. Startled, I looked up to find a tall, bronzed, blonde man standing on the threshold and regarding us with unmitigated delight. Moving forward hastily, he grasped Henry's outstretched hand.

"Well, Henry Slade, and sooner than I expected! I hope you were successful?"

Henry's smile faded. "I made some progress," he said, "though neither of the men to whom I spoke thought the time ripe for moving the goods."

His friend frowned. "Did you tell them the tariff would increase after the New Year?"

"I used every argument and more," Henry replied. "Still, they're hesitant."

"Well, that's typical, is it not? If you deal with more than one individual, there is always a difference of opinion and a wait before final accord can be reached. However, you have put them on the alert and that is certainly a step in the right direction."

"I did not travel thirteen thousand miles for a step," Henry said. "Moreover, a rival company has made a serious attempt to secure the rights."

"When?" his friend barked.

"Just before I left Boston. I was able to disassociate myself in time, but I had some difficult moments."

I had listened to this interchange with some confusion. "Are you still in the importing business, Henry?" I demanded.

For some reason, my cousin laughed shortly. "Occasionally, when I see a chance to make a profit," he answered.

"But how rude we have been to plunge into such a discussion immediately, Henry," said his friend. "Do you know that you've not even introduced me to two of the most beautiful women it has been my pleasure to see in this benighted village?" He came to stand in front of Mary and myself. "I am Charles Collier, renegade British subject and sometime pirate—but I shall not believe that either of you young ladies is the governess Henry mentioned he was seeking."

"They're not," Henry replied. "And characteristically, you did not give me an opportunity to introduce them. My cousins, Mrs. and Miss Brett—Charles Collier, wine-merchant rather than pirate."

"An interchangeable occupation," murmured Mr. Collier. He smiled at us. "They look no more like your cousins than your governesses."

To my surprise, Mary's eyes fairly flashed as she said shortly, "I assure you, sir, that my daughter and I are related by marriage and by blood to Mr. Slade."

"Your daughter!" Mr. Collier's eyebrows were half-moons against his tanned skin. "No, now you are asking me to swallow far too large a camel, Mrs. Brett."

"Step . . ." I started to amend, but Henry, laughing, explained the situation to Mr. Collier. He received a doubtful look from his friend.

"The blind leading the blind," he said, and though he spoke lightly enough, Mary frowned.

"You are suggesting I am not a fit chaperone for Ada?" she demanded.

To my barely concealed delight, he nodded. "You must know that you are not, Mrs. Brett." I was not quite so pleased with the latter half of his observation. "The term chaperone brings to my mind a grim female of indeterminate years—not a beautiful young lady. You must know that you are entering a land of most accomplished rogues."

"Come, Charles." Henry looked annoyed. "You mustn't frighten Mrs. Brett. My wife and I shall be able to give her adequate protection."

A gleam of sardonic amusement flickered briefly in Mr. Collier's eyes. "You'll be asking the lovely and sprightly Doña Pilar to chaperone the chaperone? Interesting."

"She's not as you remember her," Henry said quickly. "She's grown most responsible."

"How fortunate for you, Henry. She's become a settled Spanish matron, then?" As Henry nodded, Mr. Collier said sweetly, "She must now possess *all* the virtues."

I found this exchange not quite pleasant. Until that moment, Pilar de Villeneuva y Moncado had still been the fairy princess of my childhood. Now I found myself wondering how she would receive us. Undoubtedly the presence of Mary Booth would complicate what would have been a very simple situation. I said, "Doña Pilar will find I do not really need a chaperone. I'd intended to teach in Boston and I should have lived there alone." I flung Mary a challenging look.

She said quietly, "Boston is not Monterey."

"No, Mrs. Brett, it is certainly not," Charles Collier agreed. "But I've neglected my duties as a host again—I've not offered you any refreshment and surely you must be in need of it after your ride from the harbor. I hope you'll partake of a little fruit and wine?"

"Wine?" Mary shook her head. "Water would prove more refreshing, I think."

I was not really fond of wine, but I needed to declare my independence. I said, "I should prefer wine, Mr. Collier."

He smiled at me and said to Mary, "You'd be advised to prefer it, too, Mrs. Brett, especially in Chile."

"Wine is much safer than water here," Henry agreed.

It was also unexpectedly delicious. Much of the wine I had drunk at home had been dry and as sour as vinegar, but this was nectar-sweet. Delicious, too, were some of the largest oranges I had ever seen. I had not realized how very hungry and thirsty I had been until I sat down at Mr. Collier's table. I drank more wine and was pleased when his servant filled my glass again.

"Ada,"—Mary, who was sitting next to me, spoke with scarcely a breath of sound—"sip, don't gulp. You're not used to this wine."

I gave her a cool stare. "I am quite capable of ascertaining my capacities, Mary," I said, defiantly lifting my glass and drinking deeply.

She shot me an exasperated look. "As you choose, only remember—wine is not water."

"I know that too," I replied loftily, taking another hearty swallow and setting down my empty glass with a bang that I felt emphasized my point.

"Might I give you more, Miss Ada?" It was Mr. Collier who tipped the pitcher toward me this time.

Mary put her hand over my glass. "No more, please," she said firmly.

Her action infuriated me. Turning on her, I said, "I don' need a sh-sha-shaperon." I wriggled my tongue experimentally, wondering why it felt so thick and strange, then added, "I wan' more—mush more . . . is mush besser'n washer." Really, my tongue did feel odd. I touched it with my finger.

Mr. Collier gave me a penetrating look and set the pitcher down without filling my glass. "Perhaps you'd like an orange instead, Miss Ada," he said gently.

"I am thirsy not hungry," I told him. Oddly enough, he seemed to have developed a double edge—as if there were two of him, one superimposed on the other but striving to break free. I found the phenomenon very diverting. I said, "You're twinsh."

"She ought to lie down for a little while," Mary said.

"I am thirsy not sleepy," I averred, pushing my glass toward Mr. Collier. I must have given it a too hearty a shove for it spun across the table and shattered on the floor. "Ohhhhh . . . " I said. "Sorry."

To my amazement, Henry suddenly appeared behind me, which was also odd because I had not seen him leave his chair. In a voice shaking with suppressed laughter, he said, "Ada, you must rest."

"Donnwannaress," I protested vehemently. However, when he helped me to my feet, I found I did not have the strength to resist him. I felt as if my bones had turned to jelly, and instead of walking to the divan, I had to be carried. The moment I felt its hard leather surface beneath me, I realized that I was very tired. My head felt huge and inordinately heavy. My eyelids dropped, and I must have fallen asleep immediately.

A particularly large wave must have slammed against the ship, for when I awakened, my berth was rocking from side to side and I could hear the crew shouting at each other.

On getting to my feet, I was thrown down again, but as I lay on the heaving deck, I realized my fingers were pressed against cold tile rather than wet wood!

"Ada!" Mary shrieked. "Ada . . ."

I looked up to see her start toward me. At the same time, I was conscious of a strange shifting of light together with the grating squeak of metal.

"Mary!" Henry yelled.

There was a loud crash, followed by a piercing scream and a general dimming of the light except in the middle of the room, where by the glimmering of a single remaining candle, I saw that the iron chandelier had become detached from its chain and lay smouldering on the floor.

A few paces away, Henry held Mary against him, saying, "You might have been killed. God, you might have been killed!"

I heard—or thought I heard—her wail: "You should have let it happen—it would have been an easy death."

I say that I think I heard her express this curious sentiment, but I am not sure because there was so much confusion in those moments. The floor continued to move under me, and Mr. Collier, leaping to my side, half-carried, half-dragged me toward the door. As we reached the courtyard, something crashed in front of us—it proved to be a pottery jar that had stood in a niche above us on the wall. The ground was strewn with similar fragments, and of the fountain, jolted from its basin, nothing remained save a small pool of water.

It seemed much longer, but I suspect it was only a few minutes before the earth stopped shaking—or, as Mr. Collier described it, "quaking." When we had finally regained our equilibrium, he informed us calmly that it had only been a "small tremor."

"The last time we had a quake," he continued, "I had to rebuild my entire house. I don't think I'll need to do more than patch up a few cracks this time."

"No," agreed Henry. "I've seen much worse, myself."

My heart was still pounding and my throat was dry. His statement intensified both sensations. "Where have you seen worse?" I quavered.

"In California," he said casually. "However, they are generally not even as violent as this little one, so you needn't be alarmed."

"No." Mr. Collier smiled at me. "There's so much that is beautiful that you shouldn't mind a few minor upheavals."

"After all," Henry concluded, "even paradise had its serpent."

I could have wished he had seen fit to mention that "serpent" before we had set sail for "paradise," but it seemed useless to remark on it. It was, after all, too late to turn back.

When we started toward the harbor, we found considerable confusion in the city. The "small tremor" had shaken roofs off houses, overturned carts, created havoc amongst livestock and poultry, and terrified the citizenry, for we often found our road blocked by groups of people alternately telling their beads and crossing themselves, the country being a Papist stronghold. In the immediate vicinity of the harbor, most of these supplicants were women. Many of them were on their knees in the dust, beating their breasts and looking almost more frightened than the occasion warranted. Though, as I have said, I was hard put to comprehend the Spanish used in that South American port, I did manage to catch a few words. They puzzled me.

"I expect it's because they paint," I said to Mary. "The color on their cheeks cannot be natural."

"I beg your pardon?" she asked.

"Those women." I nodded in their direction.

She looked and shuddered. "Never mind them, Ada," she said in a low voice.

"It's the first time I've been able to understand any of the Spanish spoken here," I observed.

"Don't listen to it!" she ordered.

"But it's very interesting—what they're saying, I mean," I said.

"Not to you, Ada," she exclaimed, frowning.

"They think that the earthquake was an expression of heavenly wrath directed at *them*. I expect it's all that rouge."

"Rouge?" Henry stared at me. "What do you mean, Ada?"

"And," I added, "their gowns are cut rather low for daytime wear. I imagine they think God does not approve of them."

Much to my surprise, Henry burst into loud laughter. "I suppose they might," he agreed.

Mary had been very somber since leaving Mr. Collier's house, but there was actually a twinkle in her eye as she said to Henry, "You see, she does need me."

The laughter faded from his eyes. "We both do," he said.

She gave him a startled look. "You are—kind," she said repressively, and she turned from him abruptly—but not before I had seen the flush that stained her cheeks.

I was filled with an anger I had difficulty suppressing. I longed to rip away her sable garments, for surely they were nothing but hypocrisy. Her grief for my father's passing had been of very short duration. In four months' time, she had transferred her affection to my cousin, and he seemed to reciprocate those feelings. Had both of them forgotten he was a married man?

It was a relief to open my diary that night. It took me a good two hours to record the events of the day. I began with our visit to Mr. Collier's house and its horrifying aftermath, but when I finally laid down my pen and read what I had written, I found I had devoted a great deal more space to speculating about the possible relationship between my stepmother and my cousin. The more I thought about it, the more angry I became, because I remembered that Mary had met my cousin at precisely the same time I had made his acquaintance—at my father's funeral. Had that been the reason she had insisted on accompanying me to California?

We left Valparaiso on August 3rd, and besides our occasional sightings of whales, our exchanges with other ships, and the usual meteorological complications, nothing of great moment occurred during the following month. I did notice that as the days passed and the idea of an eventual conclusion to our long voyage became less vision than reality, Henry became both uncommunicative and restless, spending long hours striding up and down the deck. It seemed to me that he deliberately avoided Mary—or, possibly, it was the other way around, though I doubted it.

It was on September 6th that we heard the cry "Land ho!"—and though I duly wrote about my first sighting of the California coast, I do not believe that I even approximated the emotions I experienced at the time. I cried. I laughed. I jumped up and down like a child at her first party, and then, as we drew closer, I fell silent, looking at the high cliffs topped with wind-flattened trees, the golden sands, the absolutely azure sky. All tedium, all anger, forgotten, I held out my arms to this beautiful new country and I said to Henry, who stood next to me, "Oh, thank you, thank you, thank you!"

Part Three

The sense of exultation that had arisen in me at my first sight of the California coastline carried me through the day and a half it took to arrive at the Bay of Monterey. Buoyed up by the beauty of that harbor, with its vivid emerald waters, its lengthy stretch of white-gold sand, its rim of pine-crested hills, I did not even mind the annoyance of losing my cape, then finding it again, or of nearly falling into the sea as I followed Mary down the rope ladder into the boat that was to take us ashore, or of feeling wretchedly unwell during our short journey across the choppy waters to land.

Oh, it was such a relief to be deposited on the beach! Even the little wave that soaked my shoes and the hem of the skirt I had carelessly neglected to lift, was welcome. It proved I was really on land! I bade farewell to Mr. Philips and the men who had rowed us ashore, and then, moving a little apart from them, I stretched out my arms to that mercifully distant ship and in the words of my favorite historical heroine, Lady Jane Grey, I cried, "And now good people, Jane Dudley bids you a long farewell. Farewell, farewell forever more!" No sooner had those words left my lips than I shivered slightly, wanting to unsay them. Just after uttering them, Lady Jane had gone to her death. I was facing a new life. Though I was not really superstitious, still I wished that I had chosen a different quotation.

Behind me, Mary laughed. "You are so literary, Ada," she observed. "All I know is Shakespeare. How is 'O precious stone set in a silver sea' for my contribution? Except that we're not on an island, we're on a peninsula." Astonishingly, she whirled around, her ebony skirts swinging high over her snowy petticoats. "Oh, Ada, can you believe that

57

we are really here?" To my surprise, she actually embraced me.

At that moment, I forgot that I disliked and distrusted Mary Booth. Laughing, I returned the embrace, "We really, really are!" I exulted. "And isn't it beautiful? It's just as beautiful as Henry said it was!"

"It really is!" Mary agreed. She paused, looking around her blankly. "Where is Henry?" she demanded.

On turning to look for him, we saw that we were being avidly ogled by a group of dark young men in bright-colored velvets. There was something singularly disquieting about the intensity of their stares. As I looked at them, I wished that I, like Mary, were wearing a black veil to obscure my features. I said, "I—I don't see him. Hadn't we better go find him?"

Mary glanced at the men. "It might be better if we wait until he finds us," she said firmly, adding in an undertone, "Pretend you don't notice them, Ada."

It was easier said than done. As I turned away, I saw several start toward us. One of them made a remark. The others laughed. I did not like the sound of that laughter. Instinctively, I backed away and with dismay felt the sand grow hard and wet beneath my feet.

Mary clutched my arm. "Stand your ground, Ada," she counseled fiercely; "you'll be in no danger, I assure you."

"Ada . . . Mary . . ." the call echoed across the beach.

"There he is!" I said to Mary with a relief I barely understood. "Henry!" I shrieked, running to him. Out of the corner of my eye, I saw that Mary was close behind me.

"Where did you go?" Henry frowned as we came panting up to him. "I thought you were following me."

It was not the time to explain the dramatic impulse that had moved me upon disembarking. I said, "Who are those men over there?"

He barely glanced at them. "They need not concern you. Come, I've seen Tom Larkin. He's asked me to bring you to his house."

Without further ado, we followed him up the cliffs. The path was steep and we were all winded when we reached the top, but still I could not gaze enough on the ocean rimmed below by jagged black rocks around which the waters churned and boiled. Masses of seaweed tentacled among them, and numerous shrieking gulls hovered over-head, searching the rock pools for food. The winds buffeted my skirts and tore at my bonnet, I should have liked to pull it from my head and let those wayward breezes tangle my hair, but the disquieting memory of those men on the beach served to stay my hand. I wished that the incident had not occurred. It had put a damper on my excitement and filled me with vague fears for which I had no name.

"Ada." Henry's voice broke into my thoughts. "Come."

I followed my cousin and my stepmother up another narrow path past what Henry termed the Custom House, a square building with a red-tiled roof and thick, cream-colored adobe walls. Tethered on a rail nearby were several horses, with high, strangely shaped leather saddles elaborately carved and studded with silver. The animals were tended by stolid dark men in shabby clothes. I did not need Henry to tell me that these were Indians. Their origin was apparent in their flat features, small dark eyes, and straight black hair. As we neared the Custom House, I caught a glimpse of silken skirts vanishing through an archway. "Will your wife be waiting for you, Henry?" I demanded.

He shook his head. "She didn't come," he answered brusquely.

I saw Mary glance at him anxiously—or was her anxiety for herself? I preferred not to speculate about it. There was too much to think about already—too much to see. By the time we had reached Mr. Larkin's house, an adobe with incongruous green shutters, the walled presidio, the plaza, the shops, and even the men and women in their vivid clothes tended to blur into an indistinguishable mass. I was dizzy from looking around me, and my feet ached. It was a real treat to enter a cool parlor, to sink onto a chair, to close my eyes and just rest until our host should join us.

Of course, I opened my eyes very quickly and felt slightly disappointed. Despite whitewashed walls and an uncarpeted floor, I might have been sitting in a New England parlor. There was the sort of furniture I had known since childhood—horsehair sofas, polished tables, a small escritoire, a pianoforte, velvet hassocks, and, on the walls, tintypes of sober Bostonians.

"I thought it would be more Spanish," I whispered to Henry.

He smiled briefly. "Mr. Larkin is determinedly Yankee,"

he said. "He married an American woman and he has remained a citizen of the United States."

"Haven't you?" I demanded, surprised.

He shook his head. "I am a Californio," he told me. There was an ironic look in his eyes as he added, "At least, that's what it says on my documents."

Before I could comment, Mr. Larkin entered the room. He was a tall man who wore a modified version of the flamboyant Californian dress. Afterward, when I attempted to describe his features in my diary, I was not sure of anything about him except his extremely penetrating blue eyes. However, I remembered his words well enough. I do not imagine I shall ever forget the shock that went through me as he said sternly, "What possessed you to bring these two young women here at a time like this? They should return to Boston by the next boat!"

The room reeled around me. "Return . . ." I gasped.

"Shhh, Ada!" Mary whispered, but I noticed she had turned white.

"Return . . . to Boston? I do not think I understand you, sir," Henry said blankly.

"Did none of my letters reach you?" Mr. Larkin demanded explosively.

"Letters?" Henry shook his head. "I received nothing in the way of communication from anyone in Monterey."

"Damn and blast it!" Mr. Larkin brought a clenched fist down on his open palm. "I wonder . . ." His eyes narrowed, then he shook his head and sighed. "It's to late for speculation. You've heard nothing of what's happened here, then?"

"I read about Admiral Thomas Catesby Jones capturing Monterey with three frigates and a cannon blast," Henry said derisively, "but I also read there'd been an official apology and a ball aboard his ship."

"That's not what I meant," Mr. Larkin said, "though it was most unfortunate."

"Most unfortunate—and most premature," Henry agreed in a low voice. "Have there been many repercussions?"

Mr. Larkin gave him a rueful look. "It left a bad taste in many mouths," he said, "but we've had other problems, too. I mean the new governor—Micheltorena."

"Micheltorena?" Henry repeated. "But I thought he was well-disposed toward Americans and . . ."

"Toward Americans," Mr. Larkin interrupted impatiently, "toward the church, and toward everybody, which makes him popular with nobody. The Californios are angry because he wants to give the church lands back to the Missions, the Missions are angry because he hasn't done it yet. The local Dons don't like the way he favors certain Yankee trappers, the Yankee trappers don't appreciate the percentage he takes, and nobody appreciates the presence of some three hundred convicts on our streets!"

"Convicts?" Henry looked at him incredulously. "I'd heard he'd recruited some of his garrison from Mexican prisons, but I didn't believe it. I thought it was a political lie trumped up by Alvarado's supporters."

"You can believe it," Mr. Larkin said grimly. "You'll be seeing them around the presidio—half-breeds with cropped ears, branded faces, and damned nimble fingers. Alvarado left a treasury stocked with exactly twenty-five cents in coin, so there's been no money for salaries. Consequently, our brave standing army will steal anything they can use— be it a chicken or a woman. There's been highway robbery. There's been"—he darted a quick look at Mary and me— "there's been—er—woman trouble on some of the outlying rancheros."

Henry leaned foward. "What of Pilar?" he asked anxiously. As Mr. Larkin hesitated, he frowned. "Has anything happened to her? She was not at the ship. . . ."

"Calm yourself, Henry," Mr. Larkin soothed. "There's no need to worry about your wife. She has her cousins to protect her." His eyes hardened. "Since you've had no news from Monterey, doubtless you don't know that the De Silva brothers are together again."

Henry's face darkened. "Felipe has returned?" As Mr. Larkin nodded grimly, he demanded brusquely, "When?"

"Close on eight months ago," Mr. Larkin said.

"And he has been at my home?" Henry scowled.

"At your home—at many homes up and down the coast of Alta California—he and his brother, Don Cruz, whom I, for one, like even less than Felipe. He's a troublemaker— they're both troublemakers, and to my mind, they're determined on making trouble. You know their sentiments when it comes to Americans."

"Or more specifically when it comes to this American." Henry tapped his chest. "Has Felipe married yet?"

It seemed to me that Mr. Larkin avoided his eyes as he answered, "Not yet, though there are plenty of women who would like to change his mind. He's come back considerably wealthier—if not wiser. He's living in his family's old home—and I hear he's looking for more property to buy." With seeming irrelevance, he added, "It is well you've returned, but as for your companions . . ."

"Sir," I said hastily, "we—er—I—am here for a purpose. I am come to instruct Henry's children."

Mr. Larkin gave me an incredulous look. "This is your governess?"

Henry flushed. "Ada has been trained as a teacher," he said. "She's agreed to work with my children." A trifle defensively, he continued, "She's young, but she's extremely competent."

"And extremely lovely, which is not always an asset in this city," Mr. Larkin said bluntly.

"She is not without adequate surveillance," Mary said softly. "That is why I am with her."

Mr. Larkin looked at her helplessly. "But you, yourself, Mrs. Brett . . ." He sighed. "I don't like it," he said to Henry, "but they're here—and if matters get worse, well, I've sent my wife and children to Hawaii. We can make similar arrangements for them."

"If it becomes necessary, sir." Henry looked at us ruefully. "I'd not anticipated . . ." he began.

"Please," I said quickly. "I am not afraid."

"Where ignorance is bliss . . ." Mr. Larkin sighed.

"But I am not ignorant. I am extremely wise," I retorted. "And I shall avoid all folly."

He laughed. "Well, you are an erudite young lady," he said indulgently. "But you must remember that Monterey is not Concord. And you must not expect the Californios to behave like the natives of New England."

"Indeed, I hope they won't!" I cried.

"Ada, dear," Mary reproved.

"Mr. Larkin gave Mary a long look. To my considerable annoyance, he said, "I put my trust in you, Mrs. Brett."

With what I can only describe as an odious smugness, Mary said, "I assure you, I shall prove worthy of it, sir."

My anger was further compounded by Henry, who nodded and said, "Mrs. Brett is a very dependable young woman."

I should have liked to tell them all that I was equally dependable and that I could not like the inference that I was flighty, but since that might have made me seem even more flighty, I held my peace. It took an effort.

Mr. Larkin smiled and said, "I expect that you'd best be on your way, Henry, if you're to reach your home by nightfall. I'll have a couple of vaqueros ride with you. Would you be needing a pistol?"

To my surprise, Henry shook his head. "I have one," he said, patting his pocket. "I hope I shan't need to use it."

"So do I," I muttered sotto voce.

Evidently it was not sotto voce enough, for Mr. Larkin gave me a sharp glance and produced a smile that was evidently meant to be reassuring, though to my mind it was rather forced. He said, "I hope I haven't frightened the young ladies too much. The incidents I have mentioned do not take place every day."

Mary shook her head. "I am not frightened."

Since she seemed to think it necessary to constantly reassert her bravery, I followed her example. "Nor am I." Yet, as I left the room, a vivid memory of my Lady Jane quotation assailed me. I hoped it had not been prophetic.

I had expected to be nervous, even terrified, during the three hours Henry said we would need for our ride to the Casa Slade. However, at the end of the second hour, I was merely very warm and not very comfortable. It had been extremely difficult for Mary and me to adjust ourselves to the motion of the conveyance Larkin had loaned us. Called a carreta, it was a rude, wooden-wheeled wagon with a canvas top. It was drawn by oxen and it reminded me of a tumbril, except that rather than being driven to your doom, you were, I decided, doomed while being driven. A silken lining and a cushioning set of down-filled pillows offered little in the way of relief from the exigencies of a rocky, pitted trail that Henry euphemistically termed "a road." Though our Indian driver seemed to have no trouble balancing himself on his high seat, Mary and I were flung against each other so often we had ceased to murmur apologies. Then there were also the strong sweaty odor of the oxen, the hot sun beating down on us, and the unwelcome attentions of assorted winged insects, including hosts of the largest flies I had ever seen!

"What time is it now, Mary?" I asked.

She scanned the little enamel watch she wore around her neck. "It's twenty minutes later with another hour to go," she sighed.

"Only twenty minutes?" I groaned. "It feels like eons."

"It's abeuonugh," she said as the cart rumbled down a deep dip in the road.

"I beg your pardon?" I screamed, righting myself.

"It's a beautiful country," she shouted, doing the same.

"Isn't it?" Henry, mounted on a nervy little chesnut, had ridden back in time to hear Mary's comment. He smiled with a proprietorial pride, obviously unaware of our discomfort. "Look over there," he continued, pointing to a grove of tall trees draped in a fall of narrow, gray-green leaves. "Those are eucalyptuses and those orange flowers beneath them are poppies. We'll be passing fields of them presently. In the spring, the hills are covered with flowers of . . ." The words suddenly died on his lips as he stared straight ahead of him at the solitary horseman blocking our path.

I was only vaguely aware of our driver's muttered command, of the sudden halt of the cart, of the shouts of the men riding behind us. I could not take my eyes off this man who had suddenly appeared from nowhere! Still as a statue, he sat on a great golden stallion. Silver gleamed on his embossed leather saddle, on his reins, his spurs, his crop. Silver threads shone from the flowers embroidered on his sleeves and his lapels. The rest was black velvet. A broad-brimmed black velvet hat was thrust on his head, shading his dark face, shadowing his darker eyes, hiding his blue-black hair that showed itself only in the sideburns that etched his cheek and in the pencil line of moustache over his full lips. He seemed more vision than reality to me—as if embodied in this one being, I looked upon the very spirit of California.

He did not have the same effect on Henry. Eyes narrowed, mouth grimmer than I had ever seen it, my cousin spurred his horse forward, saying in a grating voice, "Don Felipe."

The man before us ceased to emulate a piece of statuary. At a touch of his crop and a flick of his reins, his horse moved backward restively. "Enrico," his rider acknowledged coldly. "The seas have returned you to our shores."

To my surprise, he spoke a perfect if richly accented English.

"And you." Henry said.

"Yes." Don Felipe's mobile mouth twisted wryly. "I found it not easy to leave the land of my birth. I have not the adventurous spirit of you Americans." His hostile glance embraced the three of us.

Henry nodded. "I did not find it easy to leave California myself, but it was necessary."

"Ah, yes, necessary." Don Felipe directed another glance at Mary and me. "So I have been told. And you have brought back not one but two servants for your children."

Servants! I felt Mary stiffen, and as for me, all my incipient admiration was drowned in a wave of anger. "We are not . . ." I began hotly.

"Ada." Henry's voice cut across my protest. "I am remiss, I fear, Don Felipe. I should have introduced you to my cousins at once. Mrs. Mary and Miss Ada Brett—Don Felipe de Silva, who is also a cousin of mine, by marriage."

Don Felipe de Silva! I should have made the connection immediately, for certainly he was exactly as Mr. Larkin had described him—anti-American. I inclined my head coldly. He, on his part, bowed deeply. "Ah, I am delighted that we meet," he said courteously. "I pray that you will excuse my error." His eyes dwelt speculatively on Henry. "You see, I was told that Enrico went to seek, among other things, a teacher of the English."

"In Boston, teaching is an honored profession and one to which I am pleased to belong," I said crisply. "Teachers are not servants, Don Felipe."

His eyes narrowed. "You are the teacher?" he murmured. "How beautifully economical . . ."

"Don Felipe," Henry said sharply, "my cousins will be visiting us. If Ada wishes to devote some time to my children's education, she will, but she is under no obligation to—"

"Henry," I interrupted, "why need we explain my presence to Don Felipe? Obviously, he will believe as he chooses, no matter what he is told."

"Ada!" Mary breathed.

"Ah, there are thorns upon this little northern rose!" Don Felipe brought his restive horse a little closer to my side of the carreta, looking at me with a certain speculative interest, the first he had evinced. "You must forgive me, señorita, for my slight confusion."

I had been desperately striving to think of an answer that would pacify me and anger him. The best I could produce upon such short notice was, "Of course you are forgiven, Don Felipe. I had forgotten how very insular you Californians are. How could you know anything about the world beyond your mountains?" I smiled at him kindly and was rewarded with an icy glare.

"I have been far beyond these shores, señorita. In the last ten years I have been throughout the whole world."

"Oh?" I overlaid my words with a mild surprise. "I shouldn't have thought so."

Suddenly, surprisingly, he smiled at me. "Someday, I hope I shall have the opportunity to tell you about my travels, señorita. But it grows late and I must go. No doubt we will soon meet again." Turning to Henry, he said, "Enrico, may I be the first to welcome you and your cousins to our —insular shores. Our land is graced by your presence."

"I thank you, Don Felipe." Henry inclined his head. "Now that you, too, are home, I pray you'll not make yourself a stranger in my house."

"Of a truth, I will not." Don Felipe gave us another of his graceful bows. "Adiós, Enrico . . . Adiós Señora and Señorita Brett!" With a wave of his hand, he spurred his horse forward, disappearing in a cloud of yellow dust.

"Ada," Mary shook her head. "What could he have thought of you?"

Henry chuckled unexpectedly, "I don't care what he thought of her. It's the first time I've ever seen him disconcerted. It was a rare pleasure and one for which I was most grateful, Ada."

"I hate him," I said between my teeth. "Arrogant! Why did you invite him to your home? I never want to see him again!"

The smile fled from Henry's eyes. "Courtesy is a custom here, Ada, and I assure you—if I hadn't invited him, he would have come without my invitation."

"Why does he dislike you so much, Henry?" Mary asked. "It's not only because you are an American—it's something deeper, is it not?"

"Much deeper," Henry acknowledged. "Before I came to Monterey, he was engaged to my wife." Wheeling his horse away from us, he shouted to the vaqueros. To us, he said, "We'll be on our way—we've still several miles to cover."

"Ada." A gentle hand was on my shoulder, shaking me awake. "We've arrived."

I blinked my way out of a chaotic dream of ships, stallions, and dark-eyed Spaniards. On opening my eyes, I thought for a moment that I was still dreaming, for I was in an immense courtyard, surrounded on three sides by a sprawling adobe house. A confusion of sounds met my ears —the clattering of hooves, the thump of wooden wheels on stone, the falling plash of a fountain spray, the twittering of birds, women giggling, and over all the dull insistent roar of the distant ocean. Dizzy and disoriented, I turned to Mary, only to find that I was alone in the carreta.

"Ada, let him help you down," she said at a point somewhere to the side and below me.

Looking dazedly around me, I finally discovered her standing by our driver. "I—I've been asleep," I stuttered.

"And very soundly," she agreed. "But come, we're here."

I needed no further prompting. Now fully awake, I let the driver swing me to the ground. Barely heeding the stiffness that had invaded my legs, hips, and as the French put it, derrière, I looked excitedly at a house that even on second glance seemed palatial. A huge veranda, punctuated at intervals by wide wooden doors, was shaded by a massvie wooden balcony onto which more doors opened. It was crested by a bright red-tiled roof, partially covered by a splash of vivid purple flowers. More flowers bloomed on trees, in patterned beds, and in pottery jars. Some varieties were familiar to me—roses, sweetpeas, snapdragons, nasturtiums, hydrangeas, pansies, lilies—others evaded definition. The walls were heavy with morning-glory vines and climbing roses, pots of ferns hung at intervals from the veranda roof, and one corner of the courtyard—or patio, as I learned to call it—was devoted to a mass of those curious spiny plants Henry had pointed out to me en route and which he had called cacti. In the center of the patio, a fountain issuing from a flat basin set in a circular pool sent a spray of crystal water flashing toward a single palm tree. Nearby was a sundial, by its look far older than the house. As I gazed about me, I felt almost dizzy—it was too much to see at once; it was too beautiful. Even my initial look at the coastline and my ride through the countryside had not prepared me for the spectacle that confronted me. We had talked about "paradise," but until that moment, I realized I had not really believed in its existence.

Behind me, the giggling continued. Who was laughing in paradise? It was a moment before I discovered the Indian women grouped around an open doorway at the far end of the veranda—ostensibly, they were scraping vegetables, pounding meal in stone dishes, plucking chickens; but if their hands were automatically performing these tasks, their eyes were fixed on us. Discomfited by this concentrated, unwavering stare, I smiled and waved—their giggling increased.

"These are your cousins, Enrico?"

The words were Spanish, the voice was soft and musical and close at hand, but I had another moment of confusion before I was able to identify the speaker. Certainly, it was not one of the Indian girls. Then, in the center of the veranda under the shadow of the overhanging balcony, I saw her, standing beside Henry, looking at me and then at Mary. She was dressed in a black silk gown patterned with immense scarlet flowers, and she had thrust a red rose into her intricately braided black hair. This touch of gaiety, however, contrasted strongly with the grave, almost solemn expression in her great dark eyes.

It seemed to me that Henry, too, looked exceptionally grave as he said, "Yes, Pilar, these are my cousins—Mary and Ada Brett." He turned to us. "This is my wife," he said.

She stepped forward. "I bid you welcome to the Casa Slade," she said, still in Spanish.

"I cannot think why my letters did not reach you," Henry said, and frowned.

"You did not know we were coming?" Mary asked her quickly.

Pilar shook her head. "I did not know." She shrugged. "But that is of little moment. We are always prepared for visitors—and always delighted to welcome them."

She had more to say to us, but I barely listened to her flow of words, even though I had no difficulty in understanding her well-articulated, mercifully slow Spanish. I was far too busy with my own thoughts. I should have known, I reasoned, that the fairy princess of my childhood would be small and lithe and delicate, a brunette replica of Mary Booth, and as she studied us, I knew too, that for all her gracious acceptance of our presence and the warm grasp of her hands, she had disliked Mary Booth. No, if I were to be honest, I should have to acknowledge a chilling truth—she had disliked both of us. Nor could I discern any excitement over the advent of the husband she had not seen for something like seventeen months. Question upon troubled question arose to plague me—the more because I could not produce any answers at all.

Yet, only an hour later, I was already having misgivings about my misgivings. Lying upstairs in a large cool room with a window facing the distant hills, deep blue in the setting sun, and a door opening toward the sea, viewed through a tracery of tufted pines, I felt much more at ease. One of the Indian serving women had helped divest me of my travel-stained garments, another had brought up a tin tub, and still another had filled it with warm scented water, staying to help me bathe. Though I was unused to such attentions, I was too tired to resist them, and it was wonderfully relaxing to be washed, massaged, and put to bed as if I were a helpless child. I lay back on a down-filled mattress under cool, lavender-scented sheets and rough wool blankets. I would rest, I decided, until it was time for supper—eaten, Henry told me, at the surprising hour of eight or nine. I closed my eyes, and for the second time that day, I must have fallen asleep immediately.

I awakened suddenly, aroused by an unfamiliar sound. My cabin was filled with moonlight. I had never seen it so bright. Startled, I glanced toward the porthole and saw instead the starlit sky framed by my doorway. I laughed out loud. I had been confused again. I was no longer on shipboard. I was in my cousin's house and I must have slept far past the supper hour, but I did not feel hungry—only exhilarated because I was not on the ship, not in a tiny area I could span simply by reaching out my two arms. My room was immense and beyond it lay the whole world, risen from the engulfing waters! So might Noah have felt after the flood ended. I had a compelling desire to enjoy a little of my new freedom. Slipping from my bed, I wrapped my peignoir about me and ran onto the balcony. The evening sky was radiant! I had seen it encrusted with stars, I had seen hundreds of moons as large as the one overhead—but

they had illumined only water. The great white orb that
hung over the garden shed its silvery light on trees and flowers and the fountain, while into my ears poured a host of
wonderful sounds—frogs, crickets, the song of the nightingale, the less melodious but equally welcome hoot of an
owl, and other nameless murmurs.

"Oh," I whispered rapturously, "I love you all!" Then I
froze, for I heard another sound and knew it for that which
had awakened me—a jingle of metal on metal. Looking
down, I saw him, a slight, slender man wrapped in a long
cloak. He was standing by the fountain, staring fixedly in
front of him. Then he started to move forward stealthily.

I clutched the wooden post in front of me, scarcely daring to breathe, while through my mind ran the conversation
we had had with Mr. Larkin concerning the soldier-bandits
of Micheltorena. As I debated on whether or not to scream
and alarm the sleeping house, another figure appeared, also
slender, also slight, also wrapped in a long cape, but in aspect unmistakably feminine. I saw a small hand reach out
and draw the man into darkness.

I suddenly discovered that I was cold. Shivering, I turned
back toward my room and saw Mary, standing on the
threshold next to mine. The moonlight, falling full on her
face, threw an odd pattern of shadows across it, making
deep caverns around her eyes and hollowing out her
cheeks. Drained of all color by that pallid glow, she looked
like a ghost come back to haunt us. Her movements, too,
were ghostlike, as she silently slipped inside her chamber,
closing her door soundlessly behind her.

I did not attempt to follow her. I went back to bed, but I
did not even try to sleep. I was puzzling over the encounter
in the garden. The immediate conclusion I had reached did
not, I reasoned, have to be the right one. I might have witnessed an Indian girl slipping out to meet her lover, but as I
should have preferred to believe that most convenient interpretation, I could not. Though I had seen it only briefly, it
was impossible not to recognize that tiny figure or its dis-
tinctive way of moving—like a fluttering butterfly or a
night moth. It could only be the Doña Pilar Slade, separat-
ed from her husband for seventeen long months. A heavi-
ness above my eylids informed me sleep was returning—I
welcomed it; I did not want to think.

I dreamed I was on shipboard, becalmed on a glassy sea.

Something fell through the rigging. I did not want to look at it, but I could not avoid it. It was wrapped in a black cloak. They opened the cloak and shook it out—a dead albatross, its plumage stained with blood. They wound a rope around its neck and carried it to me. I tried to run, but I could not move my feet. I had to stand immobile while they wound it around me, around and around me, the rope with the albatross. I struggled, but the ropes held and the bird was resting on my shoulder, pressing against my neck, when I awakened into the reality of morning and a sheet that restlessness had rendered snakelike. Extricating myself from its folds, I laughed and then sobered at the thought of my dream and my experience of the preceding night. Did one have any bearing on the other? The entire subject of dreams was baffling. Did they, as the Biblical prophets of old had contended, contain an accurate reading of the future to be interpreted by an expert or were they . . . A delicious odor was seeping into my nostrils. Whence did it come?

Rolling over, I found that someone had left me a pot of coffee, a stack of those flat breads called tortillas—I had eaten some in Valparaiso and found them to my liking—a container of apricot preserves, and a large orange, split for peeling. It occurred to me that I was ravenous.

When at length, I had eaten, washed, and dressed, I emerged onto the balcony to find the sun high in the sky and the garden fairly vibrating in its heat. As the new glory of its flowering trees and patterned beds burst upon me, it seemed very hard to visualize its moonlit mysteries. Indeed, I might have convinced myself I had dreamed the whole episode. Though I knew I had not, still it seemed less daunting by day. I could believe, I wanted to believe, that rather than a secret assignation it was . . . was . . . well, something else! Impatiently, I put introspection behind me and ran down the steps into the hall.

". . . a duenna, eh? But she's not a child, that one." The words, uttered in a low furious voice, slashed through the air like a whiplash. I stood upon the last stair, transfixed as the speaker continued. "A duenna for a duenna. I find that very odd, Enrico."

"Pilar." Henry's voice was controlled but edged with anger. "I've told you that Ada is not a duenna for the children. She is a young lady of a birth as gentle as your own, who was going to be a teacher but set aside her plans to aid us."

"How very generous of her. And this . . . this other one, this Maria . . . what plans did she set aside—and why?"

"I've told you over and over again . . ."

"Ah, yes, you have told me! And is she to sit against the wall with her arms folded over her stomach, watching her stepdaughter dance at the balls?"

"I hope she will enjoy herself, while she is here. She's had sorrow enough with her father and her husband dying within two years of each other. I should think you would understand that, Pilar."

"You rend my heart," Pilar hissed. "But I should tell you, my Enrico, that old men have a way of dying."

"Pilar—Pia—how long are we to argue about this? I tell you that Mary . . ."

"I wish to hear nothing more about Maria. . . ." Her voice suddenly grew louder and nearer. I hurried back up to the balcony and descended by the stairs that led directly into the patio. I felt both annoyed and relieved. It seemed to me that Henry should have known what manner of an impression "angelic" Mary Booth would make on his jealous wife. Yet, in itself, the jealousy was reassuring, since it indicated that my suspicions of the previous night must be unfounded. Certainly, no woman involved in a clandestine intrigue would react as Pilar had to the advent of Mary Booth.

"Oh, Ada, you have had the long sleep. That is very good." Pilar emerged from the shadowed veranda, smiling as gaily as if she had never entertained an angry thought in her life.

I had wondered how I might react when I saw her face to face and what I might say. I found it amazingly easy to smile back at her and to answer, "Yes, I slept very well— straight through until this morning. Dreamlessly, too." I need not have lied about my dreams, as well, but I deemed it good policy in a household where my habitual honesty might not always be the best policy.

"Good, very good," she nodded. "A long sleep last night, a long siesta this afternoon, and you will be prepared."

"Prepared?" I echoed.

"For the dance. 'On with the dance, let joy be unconfined!' " Henry quoted, glibly turning the Byronic poetry into Spanish prose. As he sauntered over to us, I hardly recognized him. Gone were the conservative garments he had worn on shipboard. He was resplendent in blue velvet, with a scarlet sash circling his waist and heavy gold braid on both sleeves and lapels. He caught my bemused expression and laughed. "When in Rome, my dear Ada . . ."

"Is he not magnificent?" Pilar stood on tip-toes to run her small hand through his hair. "A whole seventeen months and I did not see this gold, which is rarer and more precious than any you gouge from our hills or pan from our streams. I have prayed to the Madonna that my children will have hair this color, but alas, Javier and Rosa share my black hair."

Henry looked at her strangely. "Are you—so happy to see me, Pilar?"

"Did you think I would not be, my love?" She smiled.

Evidently oblivious of my presence, he continued to regard her seriously. "I received no letters from you," he said.

"I received none from you," she countered.

"None?" He frowned. "I wrote often."

"And so did I," she said quickly, "but I have heard of mail that languishes on board ship and in postoffices for many years. Once a young man sent a proposal of marriage to a girl he loved and she received it—twenty years later."

"I know that story," Henry said. "Your father told it to me." He gave her a doubtful look. "Then—must we blame the mails?" he asked.

"If we are not to blame each other." It seemed to me that there was more than a trace of defiance in her tone. It made me uncomfortable. I decided to create a diversion.

"Isn't it time that I saw your children, Henry?" I asked. "I should love to meet them—and if I am to give them lessons . . ."

"No, we'll not speak of lessons, yet." Pilar said. "You have just arrived."

"Still, I should like to meet them," I pursued.

"They are not here," she said. "They have gone walking with your—stepmother."

"Oh?" I felt slightly surprised. "Mary took them walking?"

"They took her walking," Henry corrected with a smile. "They took quite a fancy to her."

Pilar raised her eyebrows, "I do not believe they did, Enrico. It is only that they find any stranger fascinating. I am sure they will be equally enchanted with Ada, here."

"Perhaps I will have the opportunity to find out this afternoon," I said.

"No." She shook her head. "Not this afternoon, for we will all be resting. Tonight will be very long. Do you have the bones, Ada?"

"Bones?" I echoed, startled. I looked at Henry. In English, I said, "Did she mean—bones?"

He answered me in the same language. "Yes, bones." He added in Spanish, "Whalebones?"

"Yes." Pilar touched my waist. "Oh, so stiff. You are wearing them, no?"

I flushed at her mention of the unmentionable. "Yes, I am."

"Tonight, you will *not*," she stressed. "Tonight, your body must be free—so!" She moved in patterned steps, as if she were dancing to the strains of far-off music. "Otherwise, you will not be able to join us."

"Join you?" I questioned.

"In the dance, dance, dance—" She whirled around us, her skirts flying high over her slender legs. "My darling has come back to me from across the seven seas and we will celebrate with a great ball. All my friends have been invited —the Indians rode out to them last night. And—we shall be very gay, eh, Enrico?" Before he could respond, she had whirled away from us into the patio.

Henry shook his head. "I don't understand her," he muttered.

"She's happy because you're home," I said.

"No," he said in English, "there's something else. I've never seen her like this—not since we've been married. Years ago, when I first met her . . ."

"Speak in Spanish," Pilar said sharply, coming to stand beside Henry again. "I will not be shut out in my own house. I will not have you exchange confidences in corners with your women. Nor will I have my own children conspire against me!"

"Conspire against you?" Henry repeated incredulously. "What on earth do you mean?"

"You know. Why did you go so far from me for such a long time?"

"You know why I went!" Henry exclaimed. "And my cousin will teach . . ."

"And what about the other, who is so fair and so golden —and is not your cousin nor any relation to you at all? What will she teach my children—to hate their mother? Why did you let them go with her, this morning? What do you plan?"

I felt acutely uncomfortable. I should have liked to leave them to continue their quarrel alone, but even as I started away, Pilar flung herself at Henry, her anger evaporating as quickly as it had appeared. "Enrico, my love, my darling," she crooned. "I do not know what I say." She carried his hand to her cheek. "Please forgive me."

He sighed. "I don't understand you, Pilar. What has happened to you?"

"A year has happened to me—a year and 4—no, 5 months of lying in a lonely bed with only a pillow to . . ." She flushed darkly and her hand crept to her mouth. "Oh, poor little Ada," she cried. "You must forgive me, too. It is not fitting that I make such statements before you. I have put the warm color in your cheeks, yes?" She kissed me. "Oh, those bones . . . those bones and in such heat. No wonder that other one looks pale as creamless milk. We'll set the women to loosening your gowns. Excuse me, I go to tell them. Anita, Juana, Marabita!" Clapping her small hands, she ran across the veranda to the Indian women.

I looked at Henry and saw that he was watching her, a look of puzzled anger in his eyes. "I did not think . . ." he began.

"No," I agreed, "you didn't think, did you? And now what can we do, Mary and I?" I shuddered slightly at the thought, but I said it, "Sail back to Boston?"

"No," he said sternly. "You are welcome in my house. And if my wife does not accept—well, she will accept anyone I tell her to accept. A Spanish woman is brought up to abide by the decisions of the men in her family."

"All women are brought up to accept the decisions of the men in their family," I reminded him. "However, dear Henry, I can think of many instances when . . ."

"Stop doing so much thinking, Ada," he said shortly.

"Currently, you are the man in my family," I said lightly, "but I believe it highly possible that I shan't be able to obey you."

He smiled. "I'll not require it, I assure you." More to himself he added, "These tempers and tantrums. It's not like her . . . ."

"She told you what was troubling her," I said. "Your long absence . . ."

His laugh was ironic. "And if I should tell you that I do not believe my absence had anything to do with her attitude. If I should tell you that I cannot believe she cared whether I was here or not. . . . Nor do I believe in her so called jealousy. She is using that as an excuse for . . ." He broke off suddenly. "But I mustn't burden you with my problems. It's not fair. I want you to enjoy yourself. You will, you know. A California ball—it's another world. But meanwhile, what should you like to do?" He looked at me helplessly, "Should you like to ride with me this morning?"

I could see that he proffered the suggestion reluctantly. I said, "I'd much rather walk with me—by myself, if you wouldn't mind."

His relief was almost palpable, but he said, "I should go with you."

"No, please. I should like to be alone." I insisted. "To commune with nature."

He laughed. "Mr. Emerson could not have put it better."

"Or Mr. Thoreau," I said.

"Either," he agreed. "But you mustn't stray too far from the house. Keep it in sight—and close at hand—at all times. In fact, it might be better if I sent one of our Indian girls with you. . . ."

"No!" I remonstrated. "I am a creature of solitary habits."

His laughter offended me, "What novel did you take that from, Ada?"

"None," I said. "It's mine." I am afraid I also pouted.

"Come, don't be angry with me—and if it's the truth, I'm sorry for it. A pretty girl of eighteen shouldn't seek to be a recluse. Certainly not in California." He looked at me intently, "You are going to be happy, here, Ada, both you and Mary. I shall see to it."

I might have told him that it was my unhappiness he had secured by his insistence on linking me to my stepmother, but since it would have gained me nothing, I merely smiled and held my peace.

My first step outside of the patio was a revelation! Since I had been sleeping when we had arrived, I had missed the long avenue of poplar trees, the vast fields stretching toward the mountains, unbroken by steeple, roof, or track. Back of the house there was a cluster of adobes, where a number of small Indian children were rolling happily and noisily in the dirt. Beyond them, I saw the tall fence of the corral and a large pasture in which were a number of sturdy work horses and a few cows—or perhaps they were bulls, I have never been able to tell the difference. Chickens scurried through the dust, and ducks floated in a small pond. Though pleasantly pastoral, it was not the sort of nature whith which I hoped to commune. I wanted the solemn grandeur of tall trees, the cathedral stillness of the forest—in other words, I was seeking the pine grove I had seen from my balcony. I began walking in what I believed was its general location, and since I have an excellent sense of direction, I soon saw it shimmering in the heated distance. Joyfully, I started toward it.

It proved farther than I had imagined—much farther. By the time I had walked along the edge of several fields and traversed a meadow, there was still considerable ground to be covered. Meanwhile, I was uncomfortably aware of the burning sun, of pebbles in my shoes, wild oats in my stockings, and the general weight of my garments, which included three petticoats and a crinoline. Even more distracting were the "bones" Pilar had derided. Never had I had so much cause to regret my habit of reducing my waist two full inches by rigorous lacing! Coming to a full stop, I considered turning back, but even as I contemplated this course, I saw something so intriguing that I completely forgot my woes. Almost directly in front of me, though partially hidden by the sheltering trees, were the broken walls of what appeared to be a large house!

I gazed at it, entranced. In the many romances I had read, the heroines were always trysting near the ivied ruins of ancient castles or towers. I had longed to see one of these storied buildings, but they being in short supply near Concord and environs, I never had. While I could tell that this house was constructed not of ancient weathered stone but rather of mouldering adobe, I did note a shattered tower that yet held a rusty bell and walls, ruined enough to please the most discerning reader. Naturally, I had to explore it. Aglow with anticipation, I quickened my steps.

I was very nearly winded by the time I reached it and even warmer than I had been before, but proximity had not dispelled its enchantment. Through a gaping hole in the wall, I saw in the facade facing me a rotting archway, innocent of any shielding door and opening into a darkness that well could have been Stygian! As I looked at it, my fancy peopled it with legions of specters. Indeed, by the time I had recovered my breath, I had lost a little of my courage, for there was something eerie about the place. It was so silent! The encroaching pine trees seemed bereft of birds, and no vagrant breeze soughed through their spiky branches. Yet, that was probably a momentary hallucination, for a moment later, the air was filled with the humming of insects, and under my feet I heard the crackle of those dry and fallen leaves that seemed to be autumn's only harbinger in that shining land.

Girding up my skirts and my courage, I eased myself through the aperture in the wall and picked my way over ground strewn with such debris as bricks, a portion of a portico, and other anonymous chunks of masonry. Hesitating only the barest second, I stepped through the archway into an immense hall, dimly lit by a single window set high over my head. To my surprise, it was amazingly clean. A few cobwebs did stretch filmy shards over the corners, but the tiled floor, though broken in places, was nearly immaculate. Someone must have scrubbed it and recently. Did that mean the ruin was inhabited? Breathlessly, I listened for any tell-tale sound. I heard nothing. A second room, off the hall, proved to be equally spotless, but the next was largely destroyed. From it, I stepped over the threshold of a long chamber which looked as if it had once been used for dining. Through it, I saw a doorway facing an enclosed courtyard. A gleam of color suggested the presence of flowers. Going outside, I started across a tiled passageway flanked by squat columns. As I walked, my every step was accompanied by a curiously hollow echo. Twice, I actually turned to look behind me, and by the time I reached the courtyard, I felt definitely nervous—but then, I saw the garden!

Though it was wild and looked untended, it must once have been carefully planned; there was a fountain in the center, and though many had been uprooted and overturned, there were still a few flagstones suggesting a patterned walk, leading through beds of flowers. They remained. I had never seen so many varieties of roses, nor any so exquisite in their delicate shading. Patches of nasturtiums glowed orange and yellow, and giant chrysanthemums thrust their shaggy heads through a tangle of anonymous greenery. Around the moss-filled fountain pool stood tall brilliant gladioli, and a fall of wisteria vines hung over a portion of the ruined tiled roof beneath the belltower. I had no name for the ferns that grew in the shade of the magnolia tree nor for the cacti that rose treacherously from the yellowing grasses. Looking at their dull, fanged leaves, I shuddered—inherent in their presence was a parable concerning beauty, though perhaps it referred only to this one garden.

No sooner had this curious thought confronted me than I heard a sound behind me. Turning swiftly, I saw the largest, blackest goat I had ever seen, leaping in my direction, its strange, slate-colored, square-pupiled eyes glaring, its horned head lowered purposefully. Startled, terrified, I turned and ran. In front of me loomed a portion of a broken wall. I hoisted myself over it, falling full-length into the weeds on the other side. Struggling to my feet, I plunged waist-high into thorny bushes and pushed through them and through tangled grasses until I reached the pines. I continued to run, pulling myself around trunks, unmindful of low-hanging branches that batted me in the face and caught at my hair, unmindful of anything save my overwhelming desire to put as much distance as possible between me and that horrid ruin! At length, I burst into a small clearing beyond the trees, and then, because I could not take another step, I fell on my knees, trying to catch my breath.

Above me the sky with its complement of cottony clouds seemed to whirl. The treetops appeared to be leaning toward me, and there was a buzzing in my ears as well as black spots dancing before my eyes. I had to loosen my laces! Feverishly, I unbuttoned my bodice and yanked at my corset strings until they parted and I could rid myself of that viselike garment. Tossing it from me, I breathed in great gulps of air. Gradually, my laboring lungs were appeased, my disquieting symptoms abated, and I was spared the faint I had feared. However, I still felt very weak and there was a pounding in my throat. I lay back on the ground, trying to conquer my fears. Like an insane litany, the words, "You saw a goat not a ghost . . . a goat not a ghost . . ." surged through my head. Envisioning the beast, I told myself sternly that it was ridiculous, ludicrous, to be frightened by a goat—a harmless, milk-giving, barnyard goat. As a child, I had ridden in a little red cart drawn by two long-haired angora goats, white as snow. Aside from a penchant for devouring anything found in their path— from wisps of hay to Papa's spectacle case, inadvertently dropped on the road in front of them—they had been unremarkable. In the light of returning reason, I decided that my goat had been just as unremarkable. I had not been frightened by the animal itself, but by its sudden appearance from nowhere. Probably it had been lurking about behind some bushes, and if I were to go back, I would find it docilely munching leaves. However, I had no intention of trying to discover if this were true. My enthusiasm for goats—and also for romantic ruins—had temporarily been quelled.

In a few more moments, I felt well enough to prop myself up against a tree and enjoy the delicious coolness of the breeze, the first I had felt that morning. I could also admire the ocean. Seen from this distance, its cerulean waters were beguiling and its distant roar had a music all its own. I was moved to quote from Miss Heman:

> The breaking waves dashed high,
> On the stern and rockbound coast,

It is true she was talking about Massachusetts, but since I could glimpse the "breaking waves" of the Pacific foaming against the glistening, sea-seamed cliffs, I found the description apt enough. I tried in vain to think of an appropriate quotation for the tufted pines, but if there were any, it eluded me. Still, even without a quatrain, they were beautiful, and so were the ferns and assorted greenery surrounding them. I lay back on the ground, cradled in the bosom of Mother Nature, as it were, and in the immortal words of Ben Jonson I "rested in soft peace," closing my eyes against such sun as managed to penetrate that sylvan glade.

However, I had not remained in that recumbent position long before a startling sound caused me to open my eyes again. It was—I was sure it was—the jingle of a horse harness. I looked all around me, but since some of the foliage between the trees grew quite high, I saw nothing. I might have thought I had imagined it, if at that moment I had not heard the soft snort of an approaching horse! Leaping to my feet, I started out of the grove.

"Señorita . . ." a man called.

I did not look back. I began to run, but somehow my feet became entangled in my skirt and I fell sprawling. Before I could rise, I heard the clip-clop of hooves and felt, rather than saw, the animal come to a halt beside me.

"Are you hurt?" someone asked.

I looked up to find the man I had seen the previous day. In an instant, he had vaulted from his saddle and was helping me to my feet. "Ah," he cried. "Who has done this to you?"

"I—beg your pardon," I said falteringly, stepping backward.

His dark eyes were full of alarm. "No, no, no, you must not run from me," he said soothingly. "I mean you no harm, but what has happened to you? Your bodice is torn and I saw . . ."

I glanced down hastily and then flushed to the soles of my feet, or so it seemed to me. "It—it's not torn," I stammered. "It's only unbuttoned." I fastened it so quickly that I caught portions of my camisole in it.

"You did it?" he demanded, looking at me intently. "It —uh—it was not—*done?*"

"Done?" I repeated. "Who would do it?"

He expelled a long breath. "Who indeed?" he demanded rhetorically. "But"—he frowned—"what were you doing in the pine grove by yourself and half undressed?"

I could not meet his eyes. "It . . . it was so warm," I said defensively, "and . . . it pinched."

"It?" he questioned sharply.

I hesitated. I did not want to mention the word "corset." It seemed so unmaidenly, somehow. "Uh—everything. I— didn't think anyone was about." Indignantly, I added, "You should have made your presence known, sir."

"If your presence had been known to me, I should have made mine known to you," he retorted. "I did not expect to find an unaccompanied young woman in so desolate a spot. Surely, your cousin might have cautioned you against coming here alone."

I sensed a criticism of Henry in his words and I rose to his defense. "He told me to stay within sight of the house," I replied. "You can see it from here . . . well, almost. It must be over there," I gestured vaguely. "Anyway, you can see the pine grove from the house."

"Enrico has not been home for many months and he does not know which places are safe and which are not."

"But surely, his own land . . ."

"*His* own land . . ." I could not like the peculiar emphasis he gave those words but I was still too flustered to make an issue of it. "He does not know," Don Felipe continued, "that there are many strangers in this part of the country and not all of them are well-disposed toward young girls, especially beautiful young girls. You should never wear bonnets—they hide that hair which is the color of dark Spanish claret and they dim those eyes which I now find to be green as bay water."

His change of subject was startling as well as unsettling. I know I blushed again. "I—forgot to wear my bonnet," I said, looking down.

"You must continue to forget," he said appreciatively, while he leaned forward to pull my hair.

"Ow!" I exclaimed. "Why did you do that?"

"The Spanish ladies wear roses in the coiffures," he told ne, "but they do not favor wild oats." He held up a yellowed stalk. "I imagine you acquired it when you fell."

I had to laugh. "Thank you for relieving me of it," I said.

He bowed. "You are welcome—and now I shall take you back to the Casa Slade."

"Oh," I demurred, "it's not necessary. I can walk. . . ."

"Why should you walk in this heat?" he asked reasonably. "You've not even a covering for your head."

"I thought you didn't approve of bonnets," I replied.

"I should approve of a *rebozo* of fine white lace through which one would catch enchanting glimpses of dark sunshine."

I decided to ignore his compliment. I was sure he was teasing me. I said merely, "I may not wear white. I am yet in mourning."

"Ah, that is very sad. Black is not your color. I could imagine you clad in the green of the forest, or the turquoise of the waters that flow around the seal rocks, or even in the red-brown of the turning autumn leaves. . . ."

Those words, spoken in his melodious accented English, moved me as poetry never had. Yet, at the same time, they left me curiously tongue-tied. All I could find in the way of an answer was: "Color seems to mean a great deal to you, Don Felipe." I looked up into his dark eyes and having done so, I could not turn away.

"I am—very sensitive to color," he agreed. "But come—I must go." Before I quite knew what he had in mind, he had lifted me onto his saddle and swung up behind me, holding me lightly but firmly before him. *"Vamos,* Cazador!" he commanded, and like Pegasus the stallion sprang forward, fairly flying across the fields.

He set me down, just beyond the gates. "Remember that you are not to wander through the pine groves alone," he adjured me.

"I shall remember," I responded a trifle breathlessly. "You are most kind to have brought me home." I should have liked to add that I wished I lived at the other end of the world so that I might have remained on that horse, feeling the rise and fall of his chest against me. I could also have told him that my anger of the previous day had mysteriously disappeared to be replaced by . . . but I had no words to describe the emotion that had replaced them. I said, "Will you not be going inside to see Henry?"

He shook his head. "No, I shall not see Enrico at this moment, but I shall be here later in the evening." He wheeled his horse around and then drew rein again, "Ah, before I forget. This—might belong to you." Slipping his hand beneath his serape, he brought out something white which he thrust toward me with a smile I can only describe as mischievous.

To my horror, I found that he was proffering me my discarded corset! "I . . . I . . ." Wordlessly, I reached out my hand to receive it.

"Your are too slim a bird to need a cage," he said softly, and set spurs to his mount. Over his shoulder, he called, "Adiós, Señorita Ada."

I spent the remaining hour before the noonday meal trying to describe my sensations for my diary, but for the first time my thoughts did not flow easily—the stream had encountered rocks. It would be, I realized, very awkward to see Don Felipe again. I should be speechless, for what do you say to a man who has found and returned your corset? It was a situation for which I could find no comforting parallel in any of my books, and the more I thought about it, the more distressed I became. I needed no mirror to show me that I had turned as red as the "dark sunshine" clustering on my forehead.

"Dark sunshine," I wrote. "I do like his turn of phrase, but I shall never hear it again. Oh, dear."

Unbidden, an image of my Aunt Lucretia arose before me like Banquo at the feast, looking equally forbidding even without his gouts of blood. I could hear clearly all the sermons on "impropriety" that she had ever addressed to me. They had been numerous, but I felt that this incident would have left her without words and with apoplexy. I was relieved of her specter when a soft-voiced servant summoned me to the dining room.

Directly upon being seated at table, Henry's children were presented to me. As Pilar had said, they were both dark, but Rosa, who resembled her father, had his gray eyes framed with short spikey black lashes. She was not pretty, but she had an expressive little face and a wide infectious smile. Her brother, Javier, however, had features which were almost beautiful—fortunately, a firm cleft chin saved them from effeminacy. Though both children sat quietly enough in their places at a long wooden table, they favored Mary, who sat across from them, with many cautionary nods and smiles, as if the three of them shared a delightful secret.

Mary, however, had no answering smiles for them. Pale and silent, she stared into space, a melancholy expression in her shadowed eyes. I wondered if she had had an altercation with Pilar, yet since I could hardly ask her about it, I turned my attention to my meal, which was unexpectedly delicious—a peppery stew with a new and exotic taste.

"Ada"—Pilar looked up at me suddenly—"I looked for you this morning. Where did you go?"

I am sure I flushed because uppermost in my mind was my recent encounter with Don Felipe with all of its embarrassing ramifications. Certainly, I did not want to mention that. "I went for a walk," I said evasively.

"And did you commune with nature?" Henry demanded.

"All sorts of nature," I said lightly. "Including a big black goat."

"A goat?" Pilar repeated tensely. "Where did you see this goat?"

"In a deserted garden of all places—at least I think it was deserted. The house was in ruins but there were . . ." I ceased talking because both Pilar and her children were staring at me fixedly.

"She went to the House of Tears, too!" Rosa exclaimed and then clapped a hand over her mouth.

"Too?" Pilar looked angrily at her daughter. "Why did you say 'too,' Rosa? Were you there, also—at the House of Tears?"

Rosa exchanged a rueful glance with her frowning brother. "N-no," she stammered, flushing. Then she acknowledged the truth: "Yes, Mama."

Pilar leaned forward, clutching the table. "As often as I have told you you are not to go there, you disobeyed me!" she exclaimed. "Why?"

"We . . . we took the Señora Maria to see it," Javier said defensively, as he darted a pleading look at Mary. "You said you would like to see it, Señora Brett."

Mary's eyes softened as she looked at him. "Yes, I did."

"Why did you tell her about it?" Pilar demanded.

Henry gave her an exasperated glance. "I see nothing wrong in visiting that old ruin."

"It is evil!" Pilar exclaimed.

"Yes," Mary said unexpectedly. "I felt there was something wrong there."

Pilar darted a look at her. "You see," she said, "she felt it too."

Henry laughed. "Evil? And haunted by a—did you say a black goat, Ada?"

"It is haunted"—Pilar nodded solemnly—"Señora Mendoza has seen those who dwell in the House of Tears."

"Ooooh." Rosa's eyes seemed to grow much bigger.

"Señora Mendoza, the oracle of New Spain!" Henry said sarcastically.

"She is very learned, very wise," Pilar said defensively.

"Oh, yes, very learned indeed, he mocked. "Lizard's blood and bats eyes for the palsy."

Since the discussion was disintegrating into a quarrel, I

interrupted it, not so much in the interests of pacification but because I was consumed with curiosity. "How is this— House of Tears—haunted?" I asked.

"It's not haunted!" Henry snapped.

"By a man in black," Rosa said.

"By a woman in white," her brother told me.

"Which?" I asked.

"Both and the devil, too," chorused the children.

"That's enough!" Henry's hand slamming down on the table caused the dishes to rattle. "Don't encourage them, Ada. They mustn't dwell on this superstitious nonsense!"

"It's not superstitious nonsense!" Pilar protested. "It's the truth—and your cousins should know about it, so they'll not venture there again."

"Tell them about it, Mama," Rosa begged.

"Your father does not wish it," Pilar said stiffly. "And since I am bound to obey his wishes . . ."

"Oh, tell them, tell them," Henry rasped. "I imagine that they will agree with me!"

"Perhaps they will," Pilar said, "and perhaps they will agree with me." Fixing her eyes on us, she started to speak in a low tremulous voice. Her eyes were wide with remembered terrors as she recounted a tale as weird as anything I had ever read in the pages of Sir Walter Scott—yet there was no doubting her sincerity.

She told us about a great-aunt of hers—one Señorita Ysabel de Villenueva—who, with her brother Jaime, had been among the first settlers of Monterey. Jaime had built the house in the pine grove because his sister loved trees and the sound of the sea. A beautiful girl, Ysabel had been courted by all the men in the territory, but she had loved no one; seemingly, she was happy with her brother in their sequestered hacienda. It was known, however, that she was very religious and that she spent long hours in the little chapel, which, with its belltower, was a replica of one she had often visited in Mexico City. The bell that hung in it had a musical chime, and when Father Geraldo, the old priest who said Mass for the Villeneuvas, rang it, its voice could be heard throughout the whole area. One day, however, Father Geraldo could not come. He was ill, and in his place, he sent a new young priest from Aragon—Father Anselmo, who had just taken his final vows.

When Father Anselmo set eyes on Ysabel, he was

amazed at her beauty and she, in turn, thought him the most handsome man she had ever seen. Despite the fact that he had dedicated himself to his God, he fell in love with Ysabel and she with him. Though Father Geraldo recovered and returned for his appointed duties, Father Anselmo found ways to meet Ysabel in the pine grove. Then, one morning, early, when Father Geraldo was en route to the Villeneuva hacienda, he heard its chapel bell ringing loudly. Alarmed, he prodded his donkey to greater speed. When he arrived at the house, he found it strangely silent. No one came to the door to greet him, and in the courtyard, he saw none of the Indian servants. Yet the bell continued to ring. He went into the chapel. A horrid sight greeted him. Dangling from the bellrope was the body of Father Anselmo—he had been strangled. Lying across the altar was Ysabel de Villeneuva, a dagger in her heart.

"It was the devil, who had punished them for their guilty love," Pilar concluded solemnly.

Henry's smile was sardonic. "The devil or her brother Jaime?"

"It was not Jaime." Pilar shook her head. "Jaime was away on a trip—he returned many days later."

"But when did he leave for this trip?" Henry demanded. "No one seems quite sure of that."

"It was not Jaime!" Pilar exclaimed. "It was the devil who slew them. It is the devil who still dwells with them in the forest and who rings the bell—to summon their ghosts to chapel."

"But that bell was all rusted!" I said.

"Nevertheless there are nights when it rings," Pilar told me. "And then Ysabel and her lover return."

"Well, Ada, Mary, are you properly awed and frightened?" Henry inquired derisively.

"I don't like the place. I told you that," Mary said with a little shiver.

"I found the garden very beautiful," I told him.

"It was Ysabel who made the garden," Pilar averred.

"Someone must still tend it," I mused; "and someone must sweep the rooms. They are quite clean. Does anyone live there?"

"No one!" Pilar shook her head. "But sometimes Señora Mendoza goes there to look for herbs. She is not afraid of the dead."

"No, indeed." Henry laughed. "She's on very good terms with them—in common with Owen Glendower she 'can call spirits forth from the vasty deep!' But as Hotspur inquired, 'Will they come when they are called?' "

Mary turned to Pilar. Tensely, she demanded, "Is it true?"

"She has the gift," Pilar answered.

"She has the gift of making people think she has the gift, which is, in itself, a certain gift, but not the gift you mean," Henry snorted.

"Why do you doubt her so?" Pilar asked.

"Because such things are not logical. Because we are no longer living in the dark ages. Because the dead have had their day and their say and should be left in peace. Because, Pilar, you are too easily influenced by what Señora Mendoza tells you—by what anybody tells you, I sometimes think."

Before she could answer him, Rosa said, "All the Indians think Señora Mendoza has the evil eye."

"I wonder if it was her goat I saw in the garden," I said, feeling we had had enough conversation about the uncanny.

"You saw no goat," Henry assured me solemnly. "You saw the devil himself."

"You must not make jokes about him!" Pilar crossed herself. "You speak of serious matters."

"Serious rot!" Henry exploded.

I am sure the threatened quarrel would have erupted at that moment had not Javier spilled his wine. "Ah, Madre de Dios!" his mother cried. "Look at the tablecloth. You are clumsy as a grizzly bear, Javier!"

"Mama," the little boy cried excitedly, "there will be a gizzly bear and a bull chained together in the plaza tomorrow night. May we not go?

"Yes, yes, yes!" Rosa cried.

"No," Henry told them furiously. "I will not have my children watch this savage spectacle."

"But Papa," Javier protested, "we went last month!"

"Javier!" Pilar hissed.

"I didn't like it," Rosa shivered elaborately. "I wouldn't look. I put my hands over my eyes."

Henry stared at Pilar. "You took them to the arena?"

"I did not take them," she said. "A great group of us went."

"Cousin Cruz and Cousin Felipe and . . ."

"Oh, indeed?" Henry turned on Pilar.

"It was Cruz who caught the bear," she said sulkily.

"And I imagine it was Felipe who provided the bull?"

"It was not Felipe," she said angrily. "And if it were—and if he did take me to the bullfights—why should it matter to you. You were not here to escort me."

"You know very well my feelings about young children being allowed to witness such cruelty," Henry said coldly. "That is what concerns me the most, not who escorted you."

"But Papa"—protested his son—"it was a good fight. The bull drove his horns right through the chest of the bear and the bear hugged him and hugged him until his blood popped out of his skin and ran down all over his body and . . ."

"That is enough, Javier!" Henry commanded.

It was more than enough for me. Until then I had had no idea of what they meant. I wished that I were still in ignorance, because I no longer had any wish to continue eating. I looked at Mary and found that she, too, had paled.

"But would you believe," continued the irrepressible Javier, "that the bear died first?"

Pushing back his chair, Henry rose and went to stand over Javier. "Come with me," he said.

The boy looked at him, surprised and a little frightened. "But Papa . . ." he started to protest.

"Shall I carry you?" Henry asked.

"What would you do to him?" Pilar demanded.

"He needs disciplining," Henry told her.

"You are going to punish me, Papa?" Javier shrank away from him.

"But he has done nothing!" Pilar protested.

"He has disobeyed me," Henry answered. "I thought the children of New Spain were taught to mind their parents without question."

"You have been away many months, Henry," Pilar said.

"And now I am back and the sooner everyone recognizes that fact, the better it will be." Henry reached out his hand toward his cowering son. "Javier."

"But, Papa," the little boy said, clinging to his chair.

"I see I shall have to carry you," Henry said, reaching for him.

"No!" Javier rose suddenly. "I am not a baby to be carried," he said staunchly, and turning on his heel, he strode out of the room ahead of his father.

"Bravo," Mary said softly.

"Will . . . he beat him with a whip?" Rosa faltered.

"I do not know," Pilar replied. "I do not know this man who sits at the head of my table. He is a stranger to me." Her glance flickered over Mary and then she turned her attention to her food and a very welcome silence fell.

After the meal had ended, Mary and I, instructed by our hostess, went to our rooms for the siesta that would take most of the afternoon. "It is our custom during the heat of the day," Pilar explained. "And you must try to sleep, for you will dance far into the night."

"I shall not dance," Mary had told her gently.

"You will not . . ." She looked at her incredulously. "You do not dance?"

"I *may* not dance," Mary corrected. "I am still in mourning."

It seemed to me that Pilar's face brightened considerably at the news, though she said hastily, "I am sorry for that, Señora Maria. I am sure that also my husband will be sad, for he has said he wants you to enjoy yourself during the time you spend with us." She looked at me. "And you, Ada, do you not dance, also?"

It was a possibility I had quite forgotten. I looked pleadingly at Mary. "It's nearly six months," I said. "It only lacks four days."

She smiled at me. "I think it would be entirely proper for you, Ada," she told me.

In my relief, I could have kissed her—well, almost.

At around nine that night, the house was astir with excitement. For the past hour, people had been arriving. From my room, I had heard the carts rumbling up the road, and now in the patio, bits and pieces of laughing conversation drifted up to me. I could also hear the sound of a guitar and a woman singing somewhere inside the house. Her voice, though untrained and uneven, managed to be both haunting and provocative. The theme of her song was similar to many ballads I had heard at home, having to do with lost love and a subsequent decline, ending in a deserted grass-grown grave with a single rose lying on the stone. I indulged in some idle speculation as to how a decline was achieved. I imagined it was done through slow starvation, a prospect I could not envision, especially with the highly-seasoned taste of supper still clinging to my tongue. I had eaten far too much of another savory dish, of tortillas and fruit as well, and even though the waist of my dress had been widened, it felt a trifle confining. I looked wistfully at my discarded "bones." My waist was quite nineteen inches around without them and I felt very clumsy. However, there was some consolation in the fact that I could breathe more easily, and if I might still regret the sombre hue of my garments, black did serve to minimize the expanded girth of my waist; certainly, it formed an agreeable contrast to my white shoulders and modest décolleté. Furthermore, I had managed to add a touch of color with the pink camelias I had gathered in the garden. These were inserted in the lace at my bosom and pinned in my hair. Though the uneven glass of my mirror was hardly flattering, I decided I looked reasonably well. Thanks to my ramble through the fields, I had real color in my cheeks, and if some of it had strayed to my nose as well, I had remedied that with a coating of rice powder, something Mary could not fault since she also used it. Still, I was a little nervous about my daring when, as I had promised her I would, I joined her in her room.

To my surprise, I found her lying on the bed, clad only in her night-dress and peignoir. "You're not even going to go downstairs?" I demanded.

She shook her head. "I have a slight headache. I prefer to rest."

I wondered if headache might not mean, instead, heartache, but I contented myself with saying merely, "Oh, I'm sorry to hear it. Henry will be sorry, too, I fancy."

"I am sure that he will be far too occupied to notice my absence," Mary said. "Come, let me look at you, Ada." Slipping out of bed, she led me into the circle of light cast by her whale-oil lamp and looked at me critically. Under her scrutiny, I felt myself blushing.

"The—flowers," I mumbled. "I could remove them. I know that I should not . . ."

"The flowers are lovely," she said. "But the powder . . ."

"I did not use much of it," I defended. "You use it."

Her lips twitched. "I am not decrying the fact that you

used it, Ada. It's the way you applied it. You need to be much more subtle with powder. As for your hair . . ." Lifting the lamp, she bore it to the table where she had arranged the tonics and lotions she always carried with her. "Come." She indicated a chair. "Sit down, Ada, and let me help you. I want you to look your very best tonight."

For once I did not argue. Mary had a knack of arranging her own hair which I had always envied. Rather shyly, I said, "If you don't mind . . ."

"No, I shall enjoy it." she said.

Some twenty minutes later, I looked into Mary's proffered handmirror and barely recognized myself. "Oh, I—I do look so—so . . ."

"Ravishing," she said.

I had to agree with her. My hair swooped and waved about my face, and the camelia, cunningly placed half-way down my head amidst a cluster of curls, gave just the right effect. She had subtly darkened my eyelashes, and not only did the powder look natural but so did the slight dash of rouge she had insisted on adding. Despite my deadening black, my eyes were deeply green, and of course, I was responsible for their gratified gleam.

"A touch of orange water," she said, bringing out a small vial and pouring some of its contents onto a piece of cotton. "Here." She handed it to me. "Put this behind both ears and place the cotton in your bodice."

"Oh, it's a lovely scent."

"I've always favored it," she said. "Now, here is the *pièce de résistance!*" Rummaging through a small chest, she extracted a flat black case from which she lifted a painted paper fan mounted on guards of mother o' pearl, intricately carved and chased. "This came from Paris," she told me. "Papa bought it for me. Be gentle with it. It's nearly a hundred years old."

"Oh," I said, "I shouldn't take it. It's too beautiful."

"You must have a fan," she said. "And you use it—so . . ." Unfurling it, she placed it just beneath her laughing eyes. "There's a whole language of the fan, but I shan't teach it to you. I think that you might learn it of your own accord."

"Oh, Mary," I gasped. "How can I ever thank you?"

"You can thank me by having a very good time and dancing with as many young men as will ask you—which, I predict, will be many indeed!" She whirled around the room in a graceful waltz.

"Mary," I cried. "Please come with me!"

She stopped mid-step and came back to her bed, sinking down on it and shaking her head. "I may not dance and I am afraid I should be sadly envious if I were to watch."

All at once, I felt very sorry for her, nor did I think about her as my hated stepmother but rather as a girl only a few years older than myself, who must yet share many of the feelings I had. Impulsively, I held out my hands. "Mary, it's not fair!" I exclaimed. "You should be allowed to enjoy life, too."

Rising, she came to me and taking my hands in her soft grasp, she said gently, "I do enjoy it in my way, Ada. I—I have enjoyed it very much this evening." Her mouth quivered into a timid smile.

Looking into those speaking blue eyes, I felt all my silly prejudices dwindle. "We . . . we ought to be friends," I cried.

"Please," she answered. "I have always wished it."

I knew she spoke the truth and I did not think I had ever been as ashamed of myself as I felt at that precise moment. Flinging my arms around her, I said repentantly, "It's all my stupid fault that we haven't been!"

She patted my cheek gently. "I've never blamed you, Ada. I am sure that if some young woman had married my father, I might have felt much the same—and I didn't even have a mother I could remember." She drew a long quavering breath. "Oh, if only I might tell you why . . ."

A burst of laughter and a thread of music reached us through the open door. Mary moved away from me. "Ada, dear, go down and enjoy yourself. Hurry!"

"Why don't you tell me . . ."

She shook her head. "No, my dear, now is not the time. Go." She smiled, "As your guardian, I insist."

Earlier in the day, Pilar had shown me the room where they would hold the ball. It was a huge chamber located just beyond the parlor, and except for a number of chairs designated for the duennas, it had no other furniture. The floor was intricately tiled and on one of the walls hung a huge clouded mirror which, Pilar assured me proudly, was one of three in the entire peninsula. She was equally proud of another rarity—a giant, crystal chandelier, heavy with candles and dripping with prisms. It had been imported, she said, from Vienna by her late father.

As I made my way toward the ballroom, the laughter that had reached us upstairs grew louder, and so did the music, which sounded unlike anything I had ever heard. Its rhythms were compelling and beguiling, and I found I had to quicken my steps. I was actually running, but when I reached the threshold of the ballroom, I stopped short in amazement. I felt as if I had entered another world—a world of light and color and madness. Under that blazing chandelier, women in vivid silk dresses and men in brilliant velvets moved with dizzying speed through a maze of intricate steps. Flounced skirts whirled, showing glimpses of slender legs in flesh-colored stockings, long golden earrings gleamed in the candle flames, castanets clicked, heels tapped, and ever so often someone shouted *"Olé!"*

I found myself breathing quickly, seized by an excitement I had never experienced before. I longed to join the dancers, but at the same time, I knew I would never be able to emulate the voluptuous grace of the women. Looking at them, I felt clumsy and out of place. Even though I longed to stay and watch, I had turned away when Henry hurried to me.

"Ada!" he exclaimed. "How lovely you look! Come."

"No," I protested, hanging back. "I . . ."

"Come," he repeated; "you mustn't be shy." Seizing my arm, he forced me to accompany him across the floor. I was painfully aware of many eyes on me, none of them particularly friendly but all of them curious. And then—the music came to an abrupt stop. I clutched at Henry's arm.

"What's happened?" I muttered. "Have we interrupted . . ."

"Nothing's happened." He laughed. "Look at them."

In obeying him, I had a real shock. The dancers were standing absolutely motionless, but in such strange positions —girls caught mid-whirl, a man with a foot lifted from the floor, another on tip-toe, someone crouching—all, in fact, frozen in the patterns of the dance! Before I had the chance to comment on this amazing phenomenon, the music began again, and amid much laughter and clapping, the dance continued.

"But why?" I demanded.

"That, my dear Ada, is the fandango," Henry explained.

"I could never learn it!" I said decisively.

"You might, but it would take time. These people have had years of training, from childhood on. My wife is particularly adept at it." He frowned slightly. "Though of recent years, she has not participated too often in the balls. Tonight, however, she has made an exception. Look." He pointed. "There she is."

At first I did not see her, but with a strange little catch in my throat, I did discover Don Felipe, resplendent in ruby velvet, stitched with pearls and golden threads, a white satin sash about his waist, his breeches gartered in gold braid. He danced well; his movements were exceptionally graceful and at the same time marvelously controlled. His partner was equally adept. She was a tiny woman in a scarlet gown; her masses of black hair were dressed up high on a jeweled comb, and rubies glittered in her ears and around her throat. She moved her slender body voluptuously and she smiled enticingly into his eyes. It was with a considerable shock that I recognized Pilar. "She—she's very graceful." I said.

"Enrico, friend!" A small man, whose dark head barely topped my cousin's shoulder, stood before us. Looking at him, I had a vision of a Dresden China shepherd which had been on the mantelshelf in my Aunt Lucretia's drawing room. Though the man confronting me was olive-skinned and dark as contrasted with the shepherd's pink and white blondness, they both had that porcelain perfection of feature which I can only describe as dainty. The resemblance was enhanced by his attire—he wore a suit of emerald-green velvet, glittering with gold braid and embroidered with large flowers centered with pearls. In common with Don Felipe, he wore golden garters and white stockings; his small feet were thrust into black kid pumps. I was almost surprised to find that he was not standing on a teakwood pedestal. I was really surprised to learn from Henry's introduction that he was Don Felipe's brother—Don Cruz de Silva.

As I murmured a greeting, Don Cruz smiled at me, baring a faint line of the pearly teeth I should imagine my shepherd might have possessed. He said in a soft, clear voice, "I had no idea American ladies were so very beautiful."

Though his words were complimentary enough and his

smile warm, his eyes, which were an odd yellow-brown, regarded me with almost a serpentine stare. If I had been a rabbit, I thought wildly, I should have been devoured in an instant. I wanted to run from him, but instead, I heard myself promising to save him the next waltz. He bowed and smiled, then much to my relief, he left me. "Oh," I said to Henry, "I don't like him."

"No," Henry nodded. "Nor do I."

"He's not at all like his brother," I mused.

"He's not as tall, perhaps," Henry replied, "but other than that, there's little difference between them."

"Oh, I can't agree!" I said too hastily.

Henry gave me a sharp look, "Indeed?" he inquired. "From whence came this sudden partiality for Don Felipe. Yesterday afternoon, you seemed well on the way to hating him."

"I—I have no partiality for Don Felipe," I stammered. "It's just that he—well, truthfully—Don Cruz reminds me of a snake."

Henry's look was thoughtful. "Yes, I think you're right," he said finally. "But they are both snakes and equally poisonous, only Don Felipe might possibly rattle before he struck."

"R-rattle?" I repeated.

By the time Henry finished explaining about rattlesnakes, a species of serpent indigenous to the Far West, I felt oddly depressed. Though the analogy was probably accurate, I hated to equate Don Felipe with a snake. In the midst of my ruminations the fandango ended, and Don Cruz claimed his waltz. He moved as daintily as he looked, and held in his firm light clasp, I felt very clumsy and prayed I should not step on his toes. However, he proved an excellent partner and amazingly easy to follow. He steered me so expertly around the floor that by the time the music ended, I had almost begun to enjoy myself.

He had scarcely led me back to my cousin when I was surrounded by several other men, each smiling at me and each claiming a dance. None of them was Don Felipe. I was whirled around the room by an Esteban, a Marcos, an Ibrahim, an Indalecio, and a Jesus, all of whom were dressed beautifully, danced gracefully, murmured many of the same flowery compliments, and managed to be completely indistinguishable from one another. By the time I had danced with my sixth partner, I was winded and foot-sore enough to beg the seventh darkly handsome man for a respite. Even as he was pleasantly nodding his permission, I fled into the parlor and from thence made my way onto the veranda, where I sank down on a bench and removed my shoes, trying to wiggle some feeling back into my be-numbed toes.

Regrettably, I chose to speak out loud. "I suppose I am a success," I said, "but oh—my feet hurt."

To my horror, I heard a low chuckle from somewhere in the darkness. "That," a man remarked, "is the price you must pay, señorita." Of course it was Don Felipe. "It seems," he continued, coming to stand over me, "that we are always fated to meet when you have removed a portion of your apparel."

I quickly drew my feet up, dropping my skirts over them. "Shoes are not . . . are not . . ." I had started defiantly enough, but embarrassment stopped my tongue and I was extremely glad that he could not see my fiery blush.

"No," he agreed, laughing, "they are not. And you are quite correct, too. You are a success, a brilliant success. My brother was entirely captivated! He finds you enchanting," he told me.

"It was kind of him to say so," I murmured, wishing I could think of something equally pleasant to tell him about Don Cruz. At least I managed not to shudder.

"My brother is never kind," Don Felipe assured me. "And he has always been devastatingly honest."

"Oh?" I responded, endeavoring to produce a degree of pleasure at his revelation. "Your brother's not much like you." Too late, I caught the import of my words. "I—I mean—that is, I didn't mean . . ." I stuttered.

"In character or appearance?" Don Felipe's laugh was reassuring.

"Appearance," I said gratefully. "I cannot know whether you're honest or not, can I?"

"No, you can't," he agreed. "Not until you know me bet-ter. In a week, you will be able to give me your estimate of my character—or the lack of it."

"A week's a very short time, Don Felipe."

"Not if I see you every day," he said softly.

My heart began to pound so loudly that I was sure he

could hear it. "Every day?" was all I could manage to say without a quaver.

"Yes. Perhaps we will both come every day."

"Both?"

"I am speaking about my brother. As I mentioned, he was entirely captivated. We'll both be very determined rivals for your affections."

My distressing symptoms left me and in their place was annoyance. "I believe you are teasing me," I accused. "Neither your brother nor yourself could have become interested in me so quickly. It is entirely ridiculous, but quite in line with all the rest of the false compliments each man I've danced with this evening has felt compelled to pay me. It must be the custom of the country."

His ready laughter echoed through the quiet patio. "You must excuse me, Señorita Ada," he said finally, "but I was under the impression that beautiful women expected compliments."

"I abhor empty phrases," I said tartly, "and you may convey that information to your brother, too."

"You may be assured that I shall," he responded. "And will you do me the honor of riding with me tomorrow morning at the hour of—say ten?"

Remembering Henry's remarks about snakes, I suppose I should have refused, but with almost indecent haste, I said, "I should be delighted."

"Of a truth, so will I." He bowed. "And now, are your feet sufficiently rested to bear you back into the ballroom, so that you might dance with me?"

I would have given a great deal to respond in the affirmative, but I knew my limitations. Not only were my feet swollen but since my shoes were the least bit tight, they were rubbed at heel and toe, and if I were to avoid blisters, I dared not go back. I shook my head regretfully. "I am very tired, Don Felipe," I sighed. "I arrived only yesterday, you know. I am going to bed now."

"But it's so early!" he protested. "The dance will last all night!"

"It may—but I couldn't." I said firmly.

"You are the only young lady to have ever made such a shocking admission in my hearing, Señorita Ada," he said gravely. "You must learn to curb that honest tongue—or you will never prosper in California."

"I must take my chances," I replied.

"You must not take too many chances, Señorita Ada," he said seriously. "You are beautiful and innocent. It is a dangerous combination. Also it is a dangerous temptation. Remember—when you walk in the forest, or when you go any distance from this house, you must always be accompanied and never again must you remove your—uh—"

"I shan't," I said quickly. "I'm not going to wear my co— I'm not anymore."

"Very good." Amusement edged his words once more and bending down, he suddenly placed his hands around my waist. "Look," he marveled. "My fingers meet. You do not need your reinforcements."

His hands were warm on my unfettered waist and I could hear the sound of his breathing close to my ear. Twisting out of his grasp, I stood up so quickly that I nearly hit my head on his chin. "I must go, now," I said. "I am tired."

I bent down to retrieve my shoes, but he was before me, scooping them up quickly and bowing ceremoniously as he handed them to me. "Your glass slippers, Señorita Cinderella."

At least, I thought confusedly, as I took them from him, it was not a corset.

I awakened at dawn the next morning and lay listening to the twittering of the birds. While I am not of that poetic persuasion that must needs term their chirping "music," there was, I found, a certain euphony in the sounds they made. Through my half-open shutters, I glimpsed a silver slice of moon caught in a net of rose-pink clouds. I made a little face at it. I should have preferred to see the sun, for that would have meant it was closer to ten and I should be about to go riding with Don Felipe. At the same time, I remembered Henry's strictures and knew that rather than courting his society, I should be avoiding him. Still, it was possible that Henry might be mistaken about him—a man could change a great deal in the years from, well, probably eighteen to twenty-eight, for that is the age I judged him to be. If it had been his brother . . . I shivered. I was glad it was not Don Cruz who had asked me to ride.

I tried to sleep again, but counting sheep was of no avail and a phantom line of steers proved equally ineffective.

Sighing, I arose, sponge-bathed in the icy water from my ewer, and slipped into my riding habit, a garb which though severe, has always been most becoming to me. Fortunately, my feet felt much better and my boots caused me no discomfort. As I was pinning up my hair, my fingers froze in their task. I heard a bell! Was it coming from the pine grove?

A second later, I realized to my relief that it was much closer. "Bong, bong, bong . . . bong, bong, bong . . ." It went in measured groups of threes, then I counted a series of nine bongs. Coming onto the balcomy, I saw the Indians filing into a door at the end of the veranda. They wore black rebozos over their heads, and several of them had wound polished wooden rosaries around their fingers. My curiosity piqued, I hurried down into the patio and followed the last of them into a large, dimly lighted room. An odor composed of tallow and incense tickled my nostrils. Before me I saw a small altar; presiding at it was a priest, his head tonsured like a monk's. Naturally, I thought of the beautiful and damned Father Anselmo, but when this man turned toward me, I saw a flat, unprepossessing countenance dominated by a large hooked nose and small dark eyes. He was not of the type to tempt or be tempted, I decided. Looking away from him, I saw some of the guests I had glimpsed the previous night, and kneeling at the altar rail was Pilar, her head bowed and a jeweled rosary hanging from her clasped hands. As I watched, she crossed herself several times, nervously passing her rosary through her fingers. Her whole attitude suggested a singular devotion.

As the priest began chanting, I decided to go. When I emerged from the chapel, I found Mary watching from the doorway. I did not speak to her, for as I passed, I saw that her eyes were bright with unshed tears. I thought I knew the reason for her grief—Henry. Suddenly, I was very angry with him. Yet, had he really encouraged Mary to fall in love with him? Thinking back to those tedious days of the voyage, I wondered if I had not misinterpreted his attitude. It might have been my foolish jealousy that had caused me to believe him over-attentive to Mary. Perhaps he had merely been trying to be pleasant. It was, I realized, possible to fall in love without any encouragement at all—you could do it at first sight. I decided not to examine my reasons for this conclusion and I was really annoyed when

without my consciously wishing it, I had a vivid vision of
Don Felipe de Silva!

Breakfast was served after Mass, but many of the guests
had returned to bed. At table were only Henry, Pilar, the
children, and a sleepy youth who might have been Jesus,
Esteban, Marcos, Ibrahim, or Indalecio, but who was eventually introduced to me as Fernando. We sipped hot chocolate and munched on dry buttery tortillas in a silence broken only by the subdued murmurs of Rosa and Javier.
However, just as she arose from the table, Pilar turned to
me.

"My Cousin Felipe tells me he has asked you to ride at
ten this morning, Ada. What sort of mounts shall we provide for you and your stepmother?"

"My stepmother?" I exclaimed. "But she's not coming
with us."

Pilar raised her eyebrows. "But is she not your duenna?"

Henry gave her a sharp look. "Neither my cousin nor her
stepmother will ride with Don Felipe this morning," he said
coldly.

"But I—I have promised I would!" I cried indignantly.

"Without my permission?" he said.

I stared at him incredulously. *"Your* permission!" I exclaimed. "Why should I need your permission, pray?"

"I stand in the place of your father," he replied.

"Nonsense!" I retorted, glaring at him. "You said nothing about that when I agreed to come and . . ."

"I thought it was implicit in our understanding," he said
calmly. "As a young unmarried woman . . ."

"She would not be safe with my cousin?" Pilar finished
silkily, "Is that what you would tell Ada, Enrico? But if her
stepmother rides with her, it seems to me that both of them
would be quite safe. After all, Señora Brett accompanied
her for that purpose, no?"

I was in a quandary. I did not want Mary to ride with
me and at the same time, I felt it incumbent upon me to defend her. I said, "Yes, that is exactly why she came." I gave
Henry a defiant look.

"Then it is all settled." Pilar nodded. "Except, my dear
Ada, you have not yet told me what sort of horses I must
provide—spirited or gentle?"

"I shall choose their horses," Henry told her coldly.

It was, I realized, his capitulation. However, I could not

be entirely exhilarated by its implications. I felt quite as resentful of Mary's presence as if I still hated her. Yet, having won a victory of sorts, I was willing to placate Henry. I said, "If you choose, I will give the children some English instruction this morning."

His eyes lighted. "I should appreciate that, Ada. It's time they learned their mother tongue."

I could have advised more tactful ways of phrasing it, and evidently Pilar agreed with me, for she hissed, "Their mother's tongue is Spanish!"

"I do not wish to speak English!" Javier shrilled. "Only Americans speak English!"

A painful silence ensued, while Henry looked from Pilar to his son, both of whom avoided his scrutiny. "And what do you imagine you are, Javier?" he inquired in as chill a tone as I had ever heard him employ.

"I am a Californio!" Javier replied proudly.

"So am I!" Rosa piped.

"What are you, Enrico?" demanded Pilar, her eyes flashing. "Did you not swear allegiance to our flag, did you not take our religion when you took our lands?"

Henry swung around to face her. "I did not take your lands. They were, if you recall, given to me by your father."

She gave him a bitter look. "Yes," she nodded, "it is true. My father was most generous to you, Enrico. He gave you many things—including his only daughter."

Henry turned white. "Was that so much against your will, Pilar?" he said in a low voice.

She regarded him stonily. "In those days, I was a dutiful daughter. Now . . ." She shrugged.

"Pilar"—he took a step toward her—"what are you saying?"

"I am saying that the man to whom I owed my allegiance is dead," she said wildly, and turning, she ran quickly out of the room.

"Pilar!" Henry hurried after her. "Pilar, we are going to talk. . . ."

"I will not talk to you," she yelled from overhead. "I have nothing to say to you save what I have said already." A door slammed loudly, was shaken and kicked.

"Let me in!" Henry yelled. "Damn you, let me in!"

Shakily, I glanced down at the children. They were no

longer there, and Fernando had also drifted away. I was glad of that. The less Javier and Rosa witnessed of family strife, the better off they would be.

I found them in the patio, sitting on a bench and chattering animatedly. They were speaking so rapidly that I had difficulty in following them. I eventually discovered that the subject of their conversation was none other than Don Cruz, for whom they both seemed to have an inordinate admiration, if for different reasons.

"Always he brings me many bags of sweets," Rosa said.

"He is the bravest man in the world, and with the reata, he is unequaled. Always he captures the grizzly bear—with a single swing of the rope." Javier added, "He has promised me that I may accompany him on his next hunt."

"He has promised me that I may also ride with him," Rosa smiled. "In front of him, on his saddle."

"He has no time for little girls!" her brother exclaimed. "He must do great deeds."

"What manner of great deeds?" I asked.

Javier's eyes gleamed. "One day, he will drive all the Americans from California."

I felt cold, but I said calmly, "Indeed, and do you wish to be driven away from your beautiful home?"

"I shall not be driven away!" he cried hotly. "I shall aid Don Cruz. He has promised me that I shall be his lieutenant."

Patriotism compelled me to retort, "You ought to be proud of your American blood."

"I'm not. I don't have any American blood. I am a Californio like Don Cruz and Don Felipe and Mama and I shall not learn English!" Javier shrilled.

"Nor shall I," Rosa said predictably.

Looking at their hostile and obstinate little faces, I decided Henry had made a grievous error in leaving them alone for such a long time. However, I said only, "I know English is a very difficult language, but if you're determined to fight the Americans, you really ought to know it."

"I do not need to know it," Javier contradicted. "It is a dog's tongue. That is what my cousin, Don Cruz says—only dogs speak it. Woof, woof, woof!"

"Woof, woof, woof!" giggled Rosa.

"It is not as musical as Spanish," I agreed, "but how can you ever be a spy if you do not learn to speak English?"

"A spy?" Javier frowned. "I do not want to be a spy. I want to be a soldier and fight people with swords."

"Supposing you were captured by the Americans . . ."

"I would not be captured by the Americans." Javier glared at me. "They would all be captured by me."

"Either way," I said equably, "if they discussed a means of escape in front of you—or a plan for attacking the town —and you did not understand what they were saying, wouldn't you feel badly?"

"When I am grown up, I will know English," Javier said. "My father knows English."

"You will not know it unless you study it," I told him. "Poor Javier, how the American soldiers will laugh at you when they find that you don't know a single word of English. How safe they will feel."

"They will not!" he exclaimed. "Because I will know English. Because you are going to teach it to me!"

"We will start with a few common words and phrases," I said, managing to conceal my triumph.

An hour later, with the words "Gata-or-gato-is-cat-I-know. But-it-is-not-*cato*-or-*cata*-in-English-it's-just-plain-cat —yes, for-both-male-and-female-cats. If-you-wish-to-distin-guish-between them-you-may-call-cato—I-mean-gato—a-male-cat. I-don't-know why" running through my head, I went to seek out Mary.

She was in her room, lying on her bed and citing the same headache which had kept her from the dance. She looked so pale and wan that I almost meant it when on fin-ishing my explanation of why she must ride with us, I add-ed, "A cross-country gallop might prove most invigorating."

She looked at me dubiously. "You are going with Don Felipe?"

"We are going with Don Felipe," I said staunchly. "You want to be my chaperone—here's your opportunity."

"I should go with you," she nodded. "It is only right and proper that I do—but do you really want me to come, Ada?"

"Of course, I do," I responded. "Aren't we friends?"

She gave me a smile so grateful that I felt ashamed of myself for my inner reluctance. "Then I shall be glad to ac-company you, Ada," she said shyly.

However, as we sat on the veranda waiting for Don Felipe, I was not so sanguine. A riding habit became Mary; she looked even better than I did, I decided despondently. She was so daintily built, her eyes were so blue, her skin so white, her hair so golden, that she resembled a particularly beautiful wax doll. I knew I suffered by comparison, and when finally Don Felipe—resplendent in gray broadcloth stitched with scarlet and black flowers, a bright red silk bandanna wound around his head under his tilted black hat, a brilliant serape swinging over one shoulder—strode up to us, I could not help noticing that Mary with her delicate beauty and he with his darkly handsome features made a most attractive pair. Here, I reasoned dismally, was the man who would serve to turn her mind from Henry. Certainly, he gave her a most appreciative glance.

"Ah," he said gaily, "I am told I have two lovely ladies to escort. I shall be the envy of every caballero in Alta and Baja California!"

Mary did not appear to have heard him. Her eyes were fixed on a shadowed spot across the patio near the entrance to the servant quarters. Clutching my arm, she whispered, "Who is that?"

Several Indian women were working near the door, but I knew instantly whom Mary meant—she was tall and massive with features so angular they might have been carved from the cliffs above the sea. Yet, though her countenance was arresting, it was her eyes that caught and compelled you, deeply set beneath her overhanging brows, they were like twin caverns, and rather than looking at us, she seemed to be peering into our very souls.

As I stared at this awesome figure, Don Felipe actually smiled at her. "Señora Mendoza has come back from the mountains," he said.

"That is Señora Mendoza?" Mary whispered. Before he could answer her, she had picked up her skirts and darted across the patio. She halted in front of the woman, looking at her with what appeared to be delighted recognition. Señora Mendosa's reaction was equally surprising; she, in turn, nodded at Mary.

"But do they know each other?" Don Felipe demanded.

"Not unless the Señora is a world traveler," I said.

He shook his head. "To my knowledge, she has not been beyond the boundaries of Monterey."

"Mary, as you know, has never been to California," I said, watching as my stepmother turned away from Señora Mendoza and hurried back to us. "Mary," I cried as she came within earshot, "what on earth . . . ?"

She gave me a bemused glance, "She reminds me of Gwynneth," she said softly.

"Your nurse?" I repeated in surprise.

"Yes . . . her eyes . . . so deep, so gray . . . I had never thought to see such eyes again . . . in this world."

"Gray! They seemed black to me!" I exclaimed.

"No, they are gray." Don Felipe looked at Mary incredulously. "You had for your nurse such a one as the Señora Mendoza?"

Mary nodded. "For a moment, I even thought . . ." She paused, compressing her lips as if she were pushing back her words. "It is not important what I thought," she said in more matter-of-fact tones. "Please, don't let me detain you, Don Felipe."

The look in his eyes was frankly curious, but he said only, "Our mounts must be ready. I'll have the vaqueros bring them to the outer gate."

The horses Henry had chosen for us were beautiful. Mine was a palomino gelding named Lilio. He was light beige, with a mane and tail so pale it seemed almost silver-gilt in the sun. Mary was mounted on a chestnut mare named Iris. Though both animals were mettlesome and spirited, they were not too wild, and after I became accustomed to the Mexican saddle, which was shaped differently from the English type I had learned to use in Concord, I felt quite at ease. I need not have worried about Don Felipe's possible preference for Mary; he could not ride at her side, for the trails we followed were narrow, and most of the time, we were forced to go single file. It was a wonderful day for riding. Even though the sun was warm, there was a fresh breeze from the sea and the sky was so deeply blue that, in itself, it seemed cooling. The scenery increased in beauty at every turn.

Time and the subsequent events of that day tend to blur my early impressions of that morning, but with an effort, I can yet conjure up images of wind-caught flowers growing thick against golden fields; the thin elongated eucalypti, their gray-green leaves veiling their peeling trunks; tall, spindly palm trees; and the ashen blossoms of the yucca tree sentineling up a mountain. Then there was the moment when we veered near enough to the ocean to see it thrusting silvery paws of water at the rocky cliffs. A few moments later, we discovered a forest of strange stunted trees. There were many of them, twisted, gnarled and bearded with falls of furry moss. There was something weird about them—as if they had been satyrs of the woodland until, like Daphne, they had been Apollo-struck into cruel and arthritic enchantment. Yet ugly as they were, I found them fascinating and stilled my horse to stare at them.

Mary rode up beside me. "Come away from those illomened pines," she begged with a little shiver.

"But they're beautiful," I defended.

"I am glad that you can appreciate them, Señorita Ada," Don Felipe said, as he joined us. "They are beautiful, these guardians of the coast, battered and torn by the vicious winds—but brave as a lost battalion fighting to the death." His eyes grew sombre. "As perhaps, one day, we of California shall be forced to do."

Mary wheeled her horse around. "Do let's leave this place," she begged. "I don't like it. It—it's too lonely." Without waiting for our response, she flicked her crop lightly against the flanks of her mount and rode off.

Don Felipe watched her go with a little frown. "Your stepmother is a strange young woman—and so unhappy."

"How do you know that?" I asked.

"Can one look at her and not know it?" he replied. "Come, Señorita Ada, we must go after her, for she should not ride on these trails alone."

Startled, I asked, "Is there danger here too?"

"In these unsettled times, there is danger everywhere," he said gravely. "Come . . ."

Leaving the trees, we rode back the way we had come, but we saw no sign of Mary. "I wonder where she went," I said.

"She must have ridden very fast," he frowned. "I . . ." The words died on his lips and his eyes widened.

"What . . ." I started to ask and then stopped in consternation, for from out of the bushes on the side of the road, a man on horseback appeared, blocking our path. He wore what appeared to be the remnants of a soldier's uniform— there were tarnished gold epaulettes on his shoulders and a few gold buttons on his filthy blue jacket. He was small and ugly with a dark pitted face and—horror of horrors—minus both ears!

"Halt!" he commanded in guttural Spanish.

As I looked at him in bemused amazement, another man stumbled out of the underbrush holding a reddening handkerchief to his bleeding face. He, too, was clad in the approximation of a uniform, and if possible, he was even more unprepossessing than his companion. Glaring up at me, he growled, "Get off that horse, you . . ."

I did not understand the name he called me, but Don Felipe rode down on him with a yell of fury. "Get out of the way, carrion!"

To my dismay, a third man, mounted on a scrubby pinto pony, galloped up behind us. His uniform had dwindled to striped blue pants and a dirty serape draped over his bare chest. "Halt, in the name of Governor Micheltorena!" he ordered, looking at me with an expression that filled me with a cold shuddery fear I did not quite comprehend. Edging his horse up beside me, he reached for my bridal rein. "Pretty little puta . . ." His words ended in a scream as Don Felipe's whip, singing past my ear, flicked open his cheek.

Urging his horse forward, Don Felipe raised his whip again, saying, "Ada, I will deal with these pigs. Go, go quickly."

I did not have to comply with his command. Lilio, terrified by the sound of the whip or by the actions of the men —I do not know which—had plunged forward and set off in such a headlong dash that the man in front of me barely had time to pull his own horse out of the way. Why I did not fall, I have no notion, nor do I know how I managed to cling to Lilio's back as he cantered madly down the trail; but I did—and moreover, I even had the presence of mind to tug at his reins with all my strength until at length I succeeded in slowing him down to a trot.

I had covered another hundred yards or thereabouts when I heard the pounding of hooves on the trail behind me. Obeying an impulse I barely understood, I guided Lilio off the road and into a clump of trees and high-growing vegetation that admirably concealed us both from the view of anyone passing. I was nearly positive that it was Don Felipe, whom I would soon see, but still . . . A few seconds later, two of the men who accosted us rode past. With them, they had a riderless horse. A thrill of pure terror shook me as I recognized the sleek golden body and ornate saddle of Cazador, Don Felipe's stallion.

I remained in my hiding place until the sound of their horses had faded into the distance. Then I came out of the thicket and rode back the way I had come. I shall never forget my emotions during the interminable minutes that passed before I reached the place where I hoped Don Felipe might be. I was cold with apprehension, rigid with fear. His riderless horse meant only one thing to me—death. He had to be dead, I reasoned dully, for how else could they have taken the animal. At the thought of him lying cold and dead on the dusty road, my eyes blurred so that I barely saw in which direction I was heading, until I nearly passed the body huddled in the small ditch just off the trail. I glimpsed it only out of the corner of my eye and brought Lilio to so sudden a stop that he reared, snorted, and neighed loudly and reproachfully. Dismounting quickly, and winding his reins around my wrist, I went fearfully back to the ditch. To my relief, it was not Don Felipe who lay there but one of the men who had threatened us. A closer look assured me that though he had been badly cut by the whip, he was not dead—he was only unconscious. As I hurriedly backed away from him, I heard the groan. At first, I thought it had been uttered by the man at my feet, but on hearing it a second time, I realized it had come from several paces ahead of me. Looking around, I first saw nothing, then noticed a place where the bushes that rimmed the trail had been trampled. Clinging to a thorny branch was a small scrap of gray broadcloth! Rushing over to it, I found him, stretched out on the ground, his head against a tree trunk. Tethering Lilio to a bush, I ran to him and knelt at his side. His face was streaked with the blood that still seeped from a huge welt on his forehead, dangerously close to his temple. He was very pale.

"Don Felipe!" I cried distractedly.

He stirred, groaned again, and, with an obvious effort, opened his eyes, looking at me dazedly. He tried to raise himself but fell back, grimacing wryly. "Go-liath . . ." he muttered.

"Oh, God!" I wailed. "He's delirious!" I wanted to sink down and weep, but I had no time for my own emotions. I had to tend to his wound. It was still bleeding! Lifting my skirts, I tore at my petticoat, first with my fingers and then with my teeth. At length, I managed to rip off a portion, which I wound around his forehead; then I gently eased his head into my lap and, propping myself up against the tree, tried to think what I should do.

No immediate plan of action presented itself. I was, I realized, in a most unenviable position. In all the books and ballads I had ever read, it was the man who did the rescuing. I could think of several instances in which an unconscious distressed maiden had been put over a saddlebow and been borne off to an adjacent hostel. In my own recent travels, however, I had not noticed any adjacent hostels, and though Henry had once described a mission to me, adding that there were two large ones on the Peninsula, I had no idea where they were located. Furthermore, the thought of putting Don Felipe over my saddlebow daunted me. And if I did manage to get him up over the horse's neck, where could I take him? I had no notion of our location. In my passionate communing with nature, I had neglected to notice those landmarks which might have indicated the way we had come. I could follow the trail, of course, but there was more than one, and how could I be sure which would lead us back to the hacienda? I did not even know how far we had come. We had been riding for quite a while. The sun was high in the sky. I wished I knew the time, but I had not worn my watch. I hate to admit it, even now, but I thought first of Mary's little enamel watch and then of Mary herself. A cold finger of fear touched my spine.

"Mary!" I said out loud. *What had happened to Mary?*

"Maria . . ." Felipe had heard my exclamation. He moved his head restively, and looking down, I saw his eyes were open again and filled with apprehension. "Maria . . ." he muttered, anxiously.

"But . . . Maria . . ." he protested, raising a hand halfway toward me, then letting it fall back wearily as if even that effort had been too much for him.

My terror had doubled. Horrid visions of Mary's possible fate arose to confront me. She must have encountered those men—and what had they done with her, or with her body, afterward—after what?

Remembering their lascivious stares and their groping, importuning hands, I shuddered. Once, in quiet Concord, the entire town had been shocked and horrified by a ghastly murder—a young maidservant had been slain by a drunken vagrant. They had found her body in a barn. It had been "violated," a neighbor's wife had confided to my mother. Mama had refused to explain what "violated" meant, but of course the matter had been discussed at school. One of my friends, replete with keyhole research, vouchsafed a vivid description of the proceedings, whispered in installments during various recesses.

At the time, we had alternately giggled and shuddered, being unaware of the larger implications of the tale. Now, I recalled it and trembled. Perhaps Mary's body lay behind one of those bushes? Bitterly, I reproached myself for having forgotten all about her—yet, I reasoned, even if I had remembered her, I should not have been able to help her, and . . . My anguished soul-searching would have to be abandoned—I had heard something, and in a moment, I had identified the sound as that of hoofbeats, more hoofbeats, coming our way. A horseman—no, more than one! I could hail them and Felipe would be rescued. Taking off my jacket, I doubled it, easing his head onto it. Then, hurried back to the side of the road. The sound of hooves was growing louder! Then, in the dusty distance, I saw them, a whole group of small dark men in uniform! Terrified, I fled back into the underbrush, crouching beside Don Felipe, praying they would pass without seeing us. As they came pounding up the trail, I realized with cold horror that I had forgotten two things—the man in the ditch and my own horse, still tethered in plain view.

As I bent protectively over Don Felipe, I saw the pistol in a holster at his belt. Taking it out, I held it in a shaking hand. Resolutely, I determined that at least one of them would die before we were captured. Spreading my full skirts over as much of Don Felipe as they would conceal, I waited grimly, tensely.

In a very short time, they had clattered into sight and dismounted, speaking excitedly and so rapidly that again I was at a loss to understand them. They found my horse and then they discovered their fallen comrade. Several of them were scanning the area; I saw three men start toward me. Lifting my pistol, I held it before me, clutching it with both hands. As they parted the shrubbery, I cried, "S-s-stay b-b-b-back on your life!"

They hesitated, looking at me in shocked amazement. At that same moment, it occurred to me that their uniforms were much neater and cleaner than those of the men we had encountered before. Then one of the soldiers said soothingly, "Señorita Brett? There is no cause for alarm. We are from the presidio. Your stepmother gave the warning. . . ."

Incredibly, amazingly, Mary, delicate little Mary Booth, had met the renegades and escaped from them. That was what the lieutenant, who rode with me, told me on our way back to the presidio. We had left a detail of men to stay with Don Felipe until a carreta could be dispatched to take him to his brother's house, which—closer than his own ranchero—lay on the edge of town.

I had not wanted to leave him, but I had been assured by the man who had examined him that he was not badly injured. "If the blow had been nearer the temple, señorita, it would have been dangerous indeed—perhaps fatal, but he was only grazed by the stone."

"Stone?" I had repeated.

"It must have been a stone," the soldier said. "Or perhaps a club, but . . ."

"It was a stone and I fell like Goliath," Don Felipe had murmured with the ghost of a smile.

It was his smile and the look in his eyes that unleashed my prisoned tears. Kneeling beside him, I sobbed and said, "I shouldn't leave you."

He had continued to smile at me. "Come, come, no tears, Señorita Ada," he had whispered. "You are too brave to weep." Catching my hand, he held it to his cheek. "She is —very brave," he had whispered to the lieutenant, who had come to stand beside me. "She is not at all—what I—I expected. She is . . ." With a grimace of pain, he had closed his eyes.

"He has fainted!" I cried.

"No," Felipe said. "No, I shall be well soon," he assured me softly. His face was momentarily darkened by anger. "And then when I have settled with"—he bit his lips, his anger faded, and a smile was back in his eyes—"then we will meet again, little Señorita Ada."

I thought of that moment all the way back to town. Even when I finally stood in Mr. Larkin's parlor, holding Mary's hand, I saw Don Felipe's face in my mind's eye and heard his voice in my head. I barely heeded Mr. Larkin's praise. At length, however, I was able to fix my thoughts on the subject at hand—Mary's escape.

Only the barest outline of her adventure had been given to me by the lieutenant. To my surprise, she did not elaborate on it. "I used my whip," was all she would say. Evidently, she had been no more explicit with Mr. Larkin, for he gave her a most bewildered glance.

"I marvel you eluded them, Mrs. Brett," he said, "when they were able to overpower Don Felipe de Sliva."

"They threw no stones at me," she told him. "I think my actions startled them."

He looked unconvinced, but he said, "I suppose I must accept that explanation since you're here, but how did you manage to find your way to the presidio?"

She shook her head. "I don't know," she said candidly. "I rode in what I thought might be the direction of the town. I was right."

"Certainly, you had the devil's own luck!" he exclaimed.

To my surprise and his, she gave him an angry look. "Why do you speak to me of devils?" she demanded. Then, before he could answer, she put out her hand. "Forgive me —I—I am not myself," she stammered.

"And no wonder!" Mr. Larkin said. "It was a dreadful experience." Though his voice was soothing and his smile warm, I detected a puzzled expression in his eyes. I felt sorry for him. No doubt he would ponder over Mary Booth's odd behavior for quite a while. I, myself, had given up trying to understand her, or so I believed at the moment.

Though the festivities attendant on Henry's return had been scheduled to last three days, we returned to a largely empty house and the information that my cousin had demanded an end to the celebration. In view of the strained conditions between him and his wife, I could understand that. In fact, I was pleased. I was not in the mood to attend any more dances at present—nor would I have appreciated the wild sounds of revelry that would undoubtedly have reached my room. I was used to quiet, and quiet was what I coveted as I made my way across the patio to the veranda in the wake of Mary. Unfortunately, not everyone had left, and since the news of our adventure had evidently sped before us on Mercury's winged sandals, we were surrounded

by a throng of men and women, all talking at once, compli-
menting, consoling, and marveling over our escape. Bitter
remarks about the lawlessness of the town, the regrettable
condition of the roads, and the political expediency of Governor Micheltorena superseded these sentiments. Dark eyes
flashed, full lips curled, and mercifully, the ensuing diatribe
gave us the chance to steal up to our rooms, unnoticed.

Fortunately, Mary showed no disposition to talk. With a
fleeting smile at me, she whisked herself into her room, closing the door firmly behind her. I followed her example, and
without even removing my dusty, stained habit, I sank
down on the bed. Until my head touched the pillows, I did
not realize how very tired I had been, but then I had the
feeling I would never be able to rise again. I must have fall-
en asleep immediately.

I awakened to an importuning hand on my shoulder and
to a confused anger because I was being disturbed when I
wanted to sleep. Trying to brush that offending hand away,
I muttered, "G'wayleamelone."

"Ada!" Fingers pressed into my shoulder, sharp nails dug
into my skin. "Ada, tell me about Felipe, was he hurt badly? I must *know*."

Wrenching myself out of that tightening grip, I opened
my eyes to darkness, but I knew who stood at my beside.
There was no mistaking that voice. I said, "He is safe, Pilar."

"But hurt," she whispered. "Hurt badly? The man who
brought the news did not say—perhaps he feared to tell
me."

"No, not badly. They said not badly."

"They?" she hissed.

"The soldiers . . . on the road. They said it was not dangerous."

"Where is he?"

"At his brother's house," I told her.

"With Cruz? You are sure?"

"Yes, he . . ." The door of my room slammed violently.
Now, fully awake, surprise and anger vied with curiosity at
her precipitate behavior, and I leaped from my bed and
ran out onto the balcony. I saw nothing, but I heard someone running across the patio, and a moment later, the gate
opened and closed.

"Señora . . . Señora . . ." The whisper issuing out of the

darkness below managed to be both harsh and pleading.
"Come back. . . . It is too late. . . ."

I heard no response. I heard only the vagrant murmurs
of the night, but my eyes having become accustomed to the
dimness below, I saw a tall portly woman standing by the
gate. I had seen her only once before, but I recognized the
general outlines of Señora Mendoza. A second later, she
had slipped through the gates, too. In pursuit of Pilar? I
could not know. And where had Pilar gone? It was all very
confusing, but since I could expect no answers to my questions, I returned to my room.

Sleep eluded me for at least an hour, and when it finally
came, it brought me a host of fragmented dreams, each
vaguely menacing and all contributing to a feeling of
unease that persisted even in the bright sunshine of the following morning. I awakened early and lay thinking about
the events of the previous day. At first, I tried to recon-
struct them exactly as they had happened, but invariably,
Pilar's late visit obtruded and I felt again her fingers hard
against my flesh, her voice harsh in my ears. Harsh and angry. Yes, I realized, she had been angry at me. But why?
Had I not done my best to help her cousin? Her cousin. Felipe. I dropped the formal Don from my thinking. It had
been Felipe's head I had cradled in my lap. It had been Felipe who had said to me . . . What exactly had he said? I
could not quite remember. I needed a prod to memory, or
I should not get the sequence right. Quickly, I arose and
took my diary from my trunk. As I had expected, once I
dipped my pen in ink, I had no trouble setting down all that
had happened. My thoughts were orderly and each moment
was crystal-clear in my mind. I wrote and wrote until something fell on the paper, smearing the ink. I looked at it angrily. It was water, but where was it coming from? The ceiling? It was not raining! Another drop fell on the paper. I
sniffed and in sniffing knew that I was crying. Crying! Yes,
my exploring fingers found dampness on my cheeks. I had
been thinking of Felipe on the road, his dark hair filled
with dust and the darker stream of his blood trickling down
his forehead. More tears fell. I pushed aside my diary, utterly unable to account for the feelings surging through me.
I decided to blame them on yesterday's untoward happen-
ings. Naturally, I had been shaken, and I had not given way
to tears, then—I had been remarkably calm. I was having a

delayed reaction. No, I was lying to myself. There was another reason for my tears, but I did not inscribe it in my diary. I preferred not to think about it—it was utterly ridiculous. I had known him only three days!

On an afternoon a week later, I sat upstairs in my darkened room, reading that blotted entry and laughing ironically. I had neither seen nor heard from him. All I knew about Felipe—Don Felipe—I had gleaned from Pilar. She, in turn, claimed to have received most of her information from Señora Mendoza, who had possibly scryed it in her crystal ball or obtained it from the "spirits." More probably, she had plucked it from that mysterious grapevine that exists in all communities where many native servants are less than gainfully employed.

Consequently, I knew that Don Felipe had recovered from the effects of the blow in one or two days, but that since then he had remained in seclusion, seeing no one except his brother—who, for reasons best known to himself, also proved elusive. However, if no one knew why the De Silvas had disappeared from the daily round of social activities occupying the Californians, no one seemed to miss either of them—not even Pilar. In fact, she was in surprisingly good spirits. She no longer glowered at Mary nor did she bait Henry. No, that was not quite true—she and Henry might not be actively at odds, but then he had rarely been at home during the last seven days, and on the one afternoon he *had* spent in the house, he and Pilar had argued violently over a minor issue. It concerned Governor Micheltorena's insistence that the men who had attacked us on the road were not part of his convict—or, as the Californios termed it, *"cholo"*—army.

"He lies," Pilar had told Henry unequivocally.

Henry had stared at her in surprise. "Larkin says that the man they arrested was not one of Micheltorena's soldiers."

"That is what Mr. Larkin says because he prefers to believe Micheltorena!"

"You're not making sense. Why should he prefer to believe a lie?"

"Because there have already been too many incidents with the *cholos* and his friend Micheltorena might be replaced by another governor and then Mr. Larkin might not fare so well!"

"Do you imagine Mr. Larkin likes Micheltorena any better than you do?"

"I happen to believe your fine friend Mr. Larkin likes anyone he believes he can control. He could not control Governor Alvarado!"

"That pig!" Henry glared at her. "You speak as if you actually admired him!"

"He knew how to deal with interlopers—people who wanted to steal our country from us. He locked them all in the jail and sent them to Mexico."

"Innocent, harmless Yankee trappers for the most part —many of whom sickened and died on the way. You did not approve that at the time, Pilar—you were horrified!" Henry exclaimed.

"Well, perhaps he was wrong," she admitted, "but Alvarado would not have let Monterey be captured by that rascally American admiral. He would have died first."

"Of fright!" Henry retorted. Unhappily, he continued, "Have you forgotten you married an American?"

"For over a year an American forgot he had married me," she said furiously. "And in that time, Enrico . . ." She stopped suddenly.

"And in that time, Pilar?" Henry prompted.

"I was very lonely—and then I became not so lonely." With these obscure words, she flounced out of the room.

Henry looked after her grimly. "It's true then," he said, almost to himself. "Someone has . . ." He bit his lip and left the room. He had been gone the rest of the afternoon.

On rereading that passage, I sighed. My visions of my cousin's fairytale existence had been obliterated. Indeed, I often wondered why he had chosen to dwell among this alien people, or for that matter . . . Sighing, I put my diary down and glanced at my watch. Its tiny gilt hands pointed to three minutes past two. Two more hours remained of the siesta, then we would rise, change our clothes, and go down to the veranda. Mary and I might take a walk, then we would return and have supper and go to bed. Tonight, however, the procedure was different; we were to go to another ball—we had already been to three that week. I sighed again and continued with my resumé—the following morning we would rise, have our usual early and late breakfasts. I would give the children another English lesson, then we would ride with Pilar, Rosa, Javier, or any one of a number of young men who had taken to visiting me and whom I still had trouble distinguishing among because none of them was other than charming, lightly affectionate, intrinsically insincere. They were helpful only in improving my Spanish. In a week's time, I had come to understand it much better —which was helpful for I now knew exactly when to say "no." During and after our rides, I could gaze on golden fields, blue mountains, towering pines, and the azure sea— though we had had two days which had been gray rather than cerulean and filled with a pervasive fog that had pressed down upon us like a cotton shroud. Still, the previous night had been incredibly beautiful. Too beautiful, I decided, thinking about it.

A group of us had ridden down to the dunes for an evening picnic. Even Mary had been persuaded to join us. We had settled down on a gleaming white beach; in the immediate distance, there were rocks literally alive with the glistening bodies of sleeping seals. The combination of moonlight on the water, the soft glow of the campfires, the melodious songs sung by various gallants to the accompaniment of guitars played by one or another señorita, would have been singularly romantic had I been in the mood to appreciate it. I was not. I sat in the company of one Esteban—or was it Hortensio—de Morales or Montego and tried not to yawn at the pleasantries he produced from his seemingly inexhaustible store of pretty phrases.

"Yes," I had agreed, "it is a beautiful night." As I have already mentioned, it was. The three-quarter moon had been hanging in the diamond-studded heavens, and occasionally the pattern would be broken by a falling star, streaking haphazardly through the darkness. A gentle breeze had been blowing and the smell of the ocean mingled with the smoke-borne scents of roasting meat and of the adjacent pines. Only someone with no sensibility could have remained unaffected by such a setting. As my companion ultimately declared, I was that someone. My ears ached from listening to his practiced gallantry, and when we finally left that enchanted beach, I surreptitiously hugged Lilio, urging him to hurry back to the corral. Later, I lay watching the rays of the three-quarter moon, sliced into further fractions by the slanted slats of my shutters, and I wept into my pillow because I had heard nothing from that arrogant, mocking, cruel, mean, ungrateful, divinely handsome and beloved Don Felipe de Silva, whom I hated with all my heart!

Yet on this, the eighth day since our adventure with the renegade soldiers, I no longer wept. I was resigned to a life without him, and if I looked at it logically, there had never been any reason for me to consider him a part of my life in the first place—it was most presumptuous and entirely unrealistic. Our initial meeting had been anything but propitious, our second had been fraught with embarrassment, our third had been but the fragment of an encounter in the dark garden, our fourth—that catastrophic ride. And thinking about . . . I decided, I had thought enough. Putting my diary away, I lay down on my bed, but I could not sleep. I felt restless and nervous, as if something were pending, which was, in itself, ridiculous, because nothing really happened around the hacienda—at least it hadn't in eight long days! I tossed and turned for another few minutes, then I decided to dress and go outside—even if the sun were hot, even if no else was stirring, it might be pleasant to be practically alone in the patio.

I put on a new flounced dress, obligingly made for me by the Indian seamstresses. It was a silk in the pale violet which with gray had replaced my dismal blacks. I wished that green were one of the colors of half-mourning. Surely, I could have been just as sorrowful in green as I was in lavender, but convention decreed and I needs must obey. Actually, it has never seemed to me that color of the lack of it should play any significant part in the habiliments of grief. True grief is in your mind, not your clothes. I knew a woman who had hated her husband, yet when he died, she had arrayed herself in the blackest of blacks, all her fingers had been heavy with mourning rings, and his hair had been woven into a ghastly mourning brooch . . . Still, violet was better than black, I concluded. With a little pang, I remembered Don Felipe's observations on the colors I should wear.

Slipping out of my room, I went down to the veranda. The sun was hot! However, there was a small arbor in the midst of the garden which looked sufficiently shady. I slipped into it and sat down on a little wooden bench. It was cooler inside and the ghost of a breeze was stirring. It was very still outside. The Indian girls who usually chattered incessantly as they worked, were not there, nor were

Rosa and Javier, who also made their contribution to the noise—no one was there except the birds, the lizards, and the insects. It was so quiet, so unnaturally quiet, that I was filled with the sort of unease that has no place in the sun, that should be relegated only to dim twilights or moonless nights. It was the feeling that tells you that dispite all outward appearances, you are not alone, that somewhere very near you someone is lurking. The feeling grew so strong that when I saw the gate open quietly, I was frozen into immobility, but I was not surprised. With something of the fascination a mouse must experience when it looks into the eyes of a hungry cat, I watched a man come into the garden—a slim young man whom I had not seen in eight days and whom, quite truthfully, I had not missed. Don Cruz de Silva.

To my mind, his movements were very furtive. Closing the gate softly behind him, he edged along the wall toward the chapel and disappeared inside. Of course, he had every right to come to the Casa Slade—he was Pilar's cousin—but guests generally clattered noisily up to the gates, they did not slip through them like a shadow. They did not sneak into the house through the chapel. I wondered where he was going and why. I should have tried to follow him, but at the thought my courage deserted me and I was only heartily glad that he had not seen me.

Oddly, I still felt as though I were not alone—as though, in fact, I were being observed. "It's my imagination," I muttered. However, the sensation persisted, and looking up, I found that the Señora Mendoza was standing by the sundial looking at me. As our eyes met, she nodded, and a grimace that could be interpreted as a smile twisted her lips; then, silently, she too disappeared into the chapel. With a little sound that I am afraid I can only describe as a squeak, I leaped to my feet and fled back to my room, where I huddled on the bed, burying my head in the pillows.

"What is it all about?" I whispered.

I could think of no satisfactory answers.

It was only after the siesta was at an end that I gathered enough courage to leave my room again. I came down with my head still full of unanswered questions. Why had Don Cruz come? To visit his cousin? It must have been his reason—but at such an hour and so stealthily . . . And what about Señora Mendoza—would she tell him that I had been in the arbor, that I had witnessed his arrival? I shuddered. I did not like Señora Mendoza, I decided. There was something absolutely—well, arcane, about her. Yet Mary actually sought her society; she was always talking to the woman, and more than once I had seen them walking through the fields, bound I knew not where.

"Ada, how very charming you look in your new dress!" I jumped slightly and found Pilar standing near me on the veranda. Smiling gaily, she came to me, slipping her arm companionably through mine. "Yes," she said, as if well pleased, "that is a lovely dress. And you are lovely in it."

I longed to ask her about her visitor, but discretion intervened and I replied, "It's kind of you to say so."

"But I am never kind," she answered seriously. "I am extremely honest. You *are* lovely, Ada. All the young men of Monterey agree with me—they have cast their hearts at your feet, and all the young ladies I know are seething with jealousy."

"You mustn't tease me, Pilar," I said wearily. I was beginning to tire of the Spanish penchant for turning a pretty phrase at the cost of veracity.

"I am not teasing you," she insisted. Moving away from me, she faced me, looking at me very intently, "Why do you not choose for yourself one or another of our caballeros and free the other poor unlucky ones so that they will go back to their own loves. It is selfish of you to hoard them all."

"All of them may go back with my blessing," I sighed.

"Are you so hard-hearted, then?" she demanded. "You love no one, not even poor Esteban de Morales, who was so very attentive to you last night . . .?"

Well, at least now I knew his name, I thought, as I answered lightly, "I've been here only eleven days, Pilar. I can assure you that I do not lose my heart so quickly."

"Do you know, Ada, I am not sure I believe you," she said. "I have observed you lately. I have caught many pensive glances . . . many soft sighings. I know how a doctor would diagnose these symptoms—he would call you 'love sick.' "

"Oh," I exclaimed impatiently, "does no one ever think

about anything except love? Surely, there are other topics of conversation equally intriguing!"

"My dear Ada, at your age . . ." She paused, staring over my shoulder toward the gate. "But look who is here—none other than Hueso!"

I saw an elderly peon walking toward us. He was clutching a large wooden box. Smiling shyly and respectfully at Pilar, he said, "Señora Slade, I . . ."

"You have come from Don Felipe," she interrupted quickly.

The peon nodded. "Yes, señora. He sent me with this—it is for the Señorita Ada."

"For—for me?" I breathed.

"Yes, señorita."

"Ah." Pilar's eyes danced and she clapped her hands. "I was wondering when this would appear. He is very late, this time, very remiss. I believe I shall chide him for it when next I see him. He has sent you a shawl, Ada. Open it and you will see."

Taking the box from the peon, I opened it. As Pilar had said, it was a shawl—emerald-green silk, embroidered with immense golden flowers and heavy with green and gold fringe. It was one of the most beautiful shawls I had ever seen. I was almost afraid to touch it. "Oh," I breathed, ecstatically.

"You may go, Hueso." Pilar smiled at the old man. "Let them give you something to eat in the kitchen." She turned back to me, "Always, to express his gratitude, Felipe sends shawls. I have several and I can think of one or two other young ladies who have been similarly favored—and now you, dear Ada"—she pressed my hand warmly—"you have one, also. It's a pretty gesture, is it not?"

Her heedless words could have been so many lead pellets, for they stung as hard and hurt as badly, but I only smiled gaily back at her. "Yes, very pretty indeed, Pilar. I do like your Spanish customs. I must thank Don Felipe. I will put this away now—"

"But aren't you going to wear it?" she demanded.

I shook my head. "I am still in mourning." For once I was glad that binding convention was yet to be enforced. Turning, I went upstairs to my room. I thought of tearing those shimmering folds in two, I thought of many things—but at length, I merely folded my present and put it away in a chest. Then, for all I had believed I had no tears left, I cried until my eyes ached.

That night, we made our scheduled trip to the Segovia Ranchero. Mary had surprised me by consenting to join us, and we rode together in one of those carretas. I found myself thinking of our original journey to Henry's hacienda—had it been less than two weeks ago? I could hardly believe it. In that short time, I knew I had changed completely. I had very little in common with that girl who had looked on California as the fabled land at the end of the rainbow. Certainly, it was still painted in rainbow colors, but I hardly glanced at the beautiful country through which we were currently passing. Beauty is as beauty does—the purple mountains were covered with spiny cactus plants; the golden fields had their complement of nettles and, worse yet, snakes; the azure seas were inhabited by man-eating sharks. As for the flower-bedecked sward—I had already felt more than one tiny tremor, and I had talked to people who had seen whole buildings swallowed up in the occasional cataclysms that rocked the area. And as for its inhabitants with their green shawls . . .

"Ada, dear, why are you looking so fierce?" Mary demanded.

"It's a bumpy ride," I muttered.

"Oh?" Her glance was curious, but she asked no more questions, fortunately. I did not feel like talking. I was thinking of what Pilar had told me earlier in the evening. Drearily, I wondered if I should try and choose Esteban or Hortensio or Dario as my special cavalier? The idea repelled me. I hated all men. I hated the idea of another ball, too. I would not dance, I decided. I would spend the evening sitting next to Mary. In that way I would free my captive cavaliers and make everyone happy, while I myself could be miserable in peace.

I might have carried out this laudable scheme had it not been for the unique way in which the ball had been planned. It took place out of doors in an *enramada*, which was a sort of arbor, topped by a makeshift roof of woven boughs from which descended great flaps of white canvas forming a tent. The dance floor, though made from beaten earth, was wonderfully hard and very wide. When we came in, there were about forty people already engaged in a contradanza. Before I could make my way to the line of chairs where the dowagers sat, I was claimed as a partner by a dark (they were all dark) young man who introduced himself as Jacinto de Segovia. Since he was obviously related to the family, it would have been the height of bad manners to refuse him. I didn't. I smiled and accepted. It seemed to set the pattern for the entire evening. Actually, it served to take my mind off my troubles. It is very hard to concentrate on intricate Spanish dance steps and problems at the same time. Furthermore, the music, which was played on two violins and three guitars, was wonderfully catchy, especially when it mingled with the click of the castanets and the accomplished tapping of high heels. To add to the excitement and charm of the occasion, many of the men watched the proceedings on horesback, just beyond the open door of the tent, jumping from their mounts to join the dancers whenever they found a partner to their liking. Several of them found me, and at one point, I heard the clatter of hooves behind me and looked up into the soulful brown eyes of a horse! To the accompaniment of rising laughter, his rider leaped lightly to the ground, immediately in front of me, and whirled me into a waltz. Everyone clapped, the women as well as the men. Indeed, during that long evening, I saw no sign of the envy Pilar had mentioned. None of the girls who danced at my side during the jota or contradanzas appeared to resent my success; they all seemed to be sharing equally in the adulation of various caballeros. I decided that Pilar must have been teasing me, after all. I was not sure that I cared for her brand of humor.

It was very late when the ball ended, and despite the shaking and rumbling of the cart, I slept most of the way home. There was a faint pink glow on the eastern horizon when at last I tumbled into bed. I was very sleepy, but before I closed my eyes, a fragment of thought trailed across my dulling senses. I had not found one partner that pleased me more than the others, but neither had I wasted any undue concentration on Don Felipe. I did not even fall asleep with his name on my lips. As I drifted into slumber, I was laughing over the horse on the dance floor.

I awakened very late. The sun was high in the sky and the chocolate someone had placed by my bed was cold and heavy with skim. I slid from my bed and immediately crawled back; my feet ached. However, since it was alien to my New England nature to be a slug-a-bed, and since I should give the children their morning lesson, I arose. I put on another of my new gowns, a soft gray which had enough of a greenish tinge to be flattering to both my eyes and hair. I have to admit that I took out the emerald green shawl, just to look at it. If I had had more pride, I should not have thrown it around my shoulders and paraded up and down my room. If I had had more pride, I should have kept myself from stroking it as if it were a kitten to be petted and fondled. As I replaced it in the chest, I wondered if he had given *green* silk shawls to Pilar and the others? He had once praised my green eyes. Surely my gift carried with it a special significance? Impatiently, I slammed down the lid, resolving to put both shawl and man from my mind. Had I not learned that I could have an extraordinarily good time —even without the presence of Don Felipe?

The children were stitting in a dark corner of the veranda when I joined them. They had been playing cat's cradle, but as soon as they saw me, they threw away the string and ran to me, their eyes big with excitement. "Mr. Larkin was here this morning!" they chorused. "Papa rode away with him."

"Really?" I said, wondering why a visit from Mr. Larkin had excited them so much.

Inadvertently, Javier provided my answer. "There is going to be much fighting and all the Americans will be driven from California," he said happily.

I swallowed the lump that had risen in my throat and said as calmly as I could, "Is that what Mr. Larkin told your father?"

"He said two Americans had been pulled from their beds in the middle of the night and marched off somewhere—no one knows where. He said that was only part of the trouble. He said there would be worse—much worse—to come."

My palm hurt and I found I was clenching my fist. I put my hands behind my back and continued my questioning. "What else did Mr. Larkin say?"

"He said they would meet with the Governor, and then they rode away." Javier smiled. "Now I can be a spy, Cousin Ada, but you must hurry and teach me more English."

"If all the Americans are to be driven away, I shall have to leave and so will your father. Do you want that?"

"I do not want you to go!" the child said earnestly. "I do not want the Señora Maria to go, either."

"What about your father?"

Sullenly, he answered, "Since he has been home, there was a big bull and bear fight in the plaza—he would not let us go. Also we do not see Don Felipe or Don Cruz. I miss them."

"Mama misses them, too," Rosa said. "She cries and cries."

"Yes, that's true." Javier sighed. "She never used to cry. She was gay and happy and she sang all the time."

"Most of the time," Rosa corrected. "Sometimes she was unhappy."

"Not until Papa came home," Javier insisted. "When Cousin Felipe was with her she laughed all the time."

I felt cold. I tried to tell myself I was listening to childish prattle, that it meant nothing, but in the light of what Henry had told me, it meant a great deal. Pilar had been engaged to Felipe. She had married Henry, true, but how happy had they been? Yesterday, I had received some advice and something hurtful had been said about the present of a green silk shawl. Were my thoughts becoming too discursive—or too involved? I did not think so . . . I . . .

"Cousin Ada"—Javier tugged at my skirts—"shall we begin our lesson?"

Reluctantly, I abandoned my speculations. "Of course," I said. "We will begin with the words you have learned. I will say the Spanish and you will give me the English equivalent . . ."

"Don Felipe!" Rosa suddenly screamed, leaping to her feet and darting across the patio.

"Don Felipe!" Javier echoed excitedly.

He was standing just inside the gate. Hardly aware of what I was doing, I arose. As the children bounded up to him, I followed. He was paler than I remembered, and there was a small red mark shaped like a half-moon just below his temple. He did not smile at me. He looked at me gravely. "Good morning, Señorita Ada," he said in English.

"Where've you been? Oh, we have missed you so much!" Rosa cried.

"Why have you not been to see us?" Javier demanded. "Mama is not here now—she has gone visiting. Why—"

He gave them the briefest of glances. "I must speak with the Señorita Ada," he told them. "Alone."

Disappointment was mirrored in their expressive eyes, but evidently they had learned to respect his wishes, for without another word, they turned away and ran inside the house.

He took my hand. "Come," he said softly. "Let us go."

I had several alternatives. I could have refused. I could have told him I knew about his flirtation with Pilar. I could have dashed up to my room, snatched up his shawl, and contemptuously dropped it over the balcony. As it happens, I ignored these intriguing opportunities and let him lead me out of the patio and to the horse standing at the post. "Oh," I said joyfully, "that's Cazador. You've found him again!"

An inexplicable but unmistakable gleam of anger flashed from Don Felipe's eyes as he said, "Yes, I found him again." I wondered where and how he had found his horse and what might have happened to the men who had stolen him. I decided not to inquire. Nor did I make any protest when he swung me up onto the saddle and mounted behind me. Had he wished it, I should have ridden with him to the end of the world. As it happens, we went no further than the pine grove.

We did not speak during our brief ride, nor did we say anything when he lifted me down and put his arms around me, holding me tightly against him. I was glad there were no words between us—I only wanted to feel his lips on mine and in a second, I did. It was not a long kiss, but it was immensely satisfying. It bore repeating and it was repeated several times, a proceeding to which I added my own contributions. Though it was practically my first attempt at osculation, I found it was an art you could master very easily. At length, we broke apart and he looked at me somberly.

"That is why I never wanted to see you again, my beautiful Ada," he said sadly.

"Why did you see me again, then?" I whispered.

"I could not help myself," he said, almost accusingly. "Believe me, I tried not to think about you. Ah, you should hate me for that, I think—you who saved my life."

"I didn't really," I protested. "They would have found you. It was really Mary . . ."

"Do you think I do not remember what happened on the

road?" he demanded. "You with your two little hands clasped around my pistol?" He laughed fondly, and then he bore first one hand and then the other to his lips.

"I didn't think you saw . . ."

"I saw everything—only I was too weak to help you. The stone . . ."

I touched the mark. "It was a terrible blow. Does it still hurt?"

He kissed my hands again. "No, it does not hurt. All that hurts is the memory of my helplessness. It was I who should have protected you."

"It doesn't matter," I said. "You are alive. That is what matters."

"I am alive," he agreed, "but without my heart. Oh, my Ada, I did not want this to happen. It is not right—not for you or me."

"Why?" I demanded.

"There are many—many complications."

Hesitatingly, a little frightened at my temerity, I asked, "Is Pilar one of those complications?"

He flushed darkly. "Pilar is a complication," he said. "But it is not as you might think. We never— It was because of the past. For many years, I was tormented by old angers and a desire for revenge. And when the opportunity arose, I tried to take advantage of it. I was very foolish. No one should look always backward. We of California are far too prone to cling to tradition, and we do not see what harm we do to ourselves and to others." He sighed. "We see nothing—until it is too late."

His disjointed words filled me with alarm. "It is not too late, not if you have realized your—errors."

He smiled ruefully. "Ah, Ada, with you it is all so simple. You would take out your little shears and you would go snip, snip, snip, and the past would be lying in pieces on the floor. You would sweep it up neatly and no scraps would remain. But for me it is not so simple. There are scraps that the wind has snatched and blown far and wide. It is for me to retrieve them—all of them—before I can look to the future."

"I wish you would tell me what you mean!" I cried.

"I may not tell you," he said firmly, "but I may tell you that I love you."

"I love you, too," I said ecstatically.

Of course, it was all wrong. All the conventions had been flouted. It had happened far too quickly. There had been no formal period of courting, not even a serenade beneath my window, and certainly his declaration should not have been made at high noon in the very same grove where I had lost my corset and where, worse yet, he had found it. Yet, standing against him once more, held tightly in his arms, I had no complaints—no, not even when the large bird seated on a nearby branch declared his presence raucously in the time-honored manner of his species: "Caw, caw, cawwww."

To me, he sounded as melodious as a nightingale.

All too soon, Felipe said, "I must take you back. But first, have this." Reaching into his pocket, he brought out a small medallion that hung at the end of a fine golden chain. It was set with rubies and diamonds in the pattern of a holly sprig. "This has been in our family for generations," he told me. "It is made from stones found in Montezuma's mines—it belonged to an ancestor who fought with Cortes." He pressed it into my hand.

"Oh, it's beautiful," I breathed.

"Wear it inside your gown. Do not let anyone see it—not yet. Do not let anyone know that you have it."

"Perhaps I shouldn't keep it until all those scraps are found."

He laughed. "No, I want you to have it. I want to know you are wearing it and thinking of me."

"I do not need a reminder," I said, holding his hand against my cheek.

Of course, he kissed me again, and taking the medallion from me, he slipped it over my head, dropping it inside my gown. "One day, you will wear this so all may see it—and on that day, you will wear also a ring to match it. I hope we shall not have long to wait, my Ada. But meanwhile, let our love be our secret."

"I shall," I promised.

All too quickly, he bore me back to the hacienda and set me down just outside the gates. All too quickly, he disappeared down that dusty road.

I did not like mysteries, I decided, as I went slowly back across the patio. Nor did I appreciate the hint of hidden dangers that had quivered in the air between us. That they threatened many more than ourselves, I had no doubt. I did not like to contemplate those old loyalties that kept him silent. He had never made any secret of his dislike for Americans; furthermore he was closely related to a man I actively distrusted and whose mysterious presence in the chapel, the previous afternoon, still disturbed me—the more so because I had failed to mention it to anyone. I had the feeling I should have told Henry. Yet the time had passed when I could, for now, whether I liked it or not, my life was inextricably (I hoped it was inextricably) entwined with his brother's.

That the children had been quick to inform their mother of Don Felipe's visit was immediately apparent to me that evening when all of us except Henry, who was still absent, met for dinner. Scarcely had we taken our places at the table when Pilar turned to Mary with a cool smile. "Ah, Maria," she said lightly, "you must take your duties as duenna more seriously."

"As a duenna?" Mary questioned.

"When a young man comes to see a girl, it is not well that they should be alone, especially if they go beyond the shelter of the house. I am not chiding you for it, Maria—or you, Ada, believe me. It is only that in my husband's absence, I feel responsible for your welfare."

"I did not . . ." Mary began.

"She did not know about Don Felipe's visit," I explained.

"You did not tell her, Ada?"

I shook my head. "It never occurred to me."

"No? But my dear Ada, I thought you were familiar with the customs of our land. A young unmarried girl must think of her reputation." Pilar smiled sweetly at me, but her eyes were bright with anger.

"I thought it was the custom only when the man wished to pay court to a lady. Certainly, you must be aware that Don Felipe would have no such intentions toward me."

Her eyes glinted. "Naturally I know that, Ada," she said softly. "Felipe is never serious toward any one—he suffered a disappointment when he was very young and I fear it has hardened his heart."

Her complacent acknowledgement and acceptance of what she must believe to be an enduring passion enraged me. I longed to thrust my medallion in her face. Since it was a family heirloom, I was sure she would recognize it. However, I resolutely kept my hand in my lap and said, "But if his heart is hard, then surely I am in no danger, Pilar."

"Oh, no, you would be in no danger," she said; "but my cousin has a wicked way with him. He cannot resist the small flirtation. I should not wish you to—suffer needlessly, Ada. Young girls can be so vulnerable."

"Yes, that's very true." Mary's eyes were shadowed. "They are very vulnerable and can so easily be misled."

"He did not try to mislead me, I can assure you both," I said dryly. "He only wanted to thank me for having such presence of mind on the road that day."

"Then certainly you should have summoned your stepmother," Pilar told me, "for she, too, showed great presence of mind."

"I shall—next time," I said demurely.

After dinner, Mary walked with me up to my room. "Might I speak with you, Ada?" she asked.

"Please . . ." I invited her in, mentally bracing myself for the lies I should presently need to concoct. As she sat down on a chair near by bed, I said, "I suppose I ought to have called you, Mary, but you were nowhere about and he was . . . was . . ."

"Precipitate?" Mary finished, frowning.

"I suppose you might call him so," I admitted.

She gave me a penetrating look. "You know, Ada, that we are among a—foreign race, here. They are charming, fascinating, but with different values and a different outlook on life."

I gave her what I considered a safe answer. "Yes, they are different."

"You are very young, Ada," she sighed.

"Five years younger than you, Mary," I reminded her.

"Five centuries younger than I!" she exclaimed. "You know nothing about life. You've been sheltered and nurtured on your poetry, your novels. . . . You've lived among gentle, unworldy people like Mr. Emerson and Mr. Alcott and their friends. Life to them is a philosophic debate. They avoid its realities. But life is real, Ada—it does not conform to the rules laid down in story books. Trust too easily given can be sadly misplaced and misused. The sooner you learn that, the better it will be for you—you will be saved much heartache and much . . ." She shook her head, saying in a low tremulous voice, "So much can happen, so much."

I had the impression she was speaking not to me but to herself and possibly to Henry. Still, I said, "I've trusted no one in particular, Mary. As I told you, Don Felipe came merely to . . ."

Mary raised her hand. "My poor Ada, I saw you with Don Felipe this morning."

"In the patio?" I asked.

"In the pine grove," she said.

A sensation akin to that which I had experienced during the Valparaiso quake came over me. If the room did not shake, it certainly whirled. I said weakly, "What—were you doing there?"

"I'd come from the House of Tears . . ." she began.

"You went there?" I demanded, momentarily diverted. "Why?"

"That does not matter, Ada," she said crisply. "What matters is what I saw in the pine grove."

"And heard? You listened?" I asked.

She flushed. "It was unavoidable. If I'd made any movement, you'd have seen me. I didn't think you'd have appreciated an interruption, Ada."

"You said nothing about it at table."

"Should you have wanted me to say anything?"

"But you seemed surprised to learn . . ."

"It was for your own protection. And what I am about to tell you is also for your own protection, though doubtlessly you'll not thank me for it."

A little tremor of fear shook me. I found I did not want to hear what she had to tell me. I said, "Please . . . don't say any more, Mary. I shan't listen."

"You must listen," she said firmly. "I've been to the pine grove many times. . . ."

"You shouldn't go there. Felipe says it is dangerous."

"He might well tell you it is dangerous, since he's been meeting his cousin Pilar there—and at the House of Tears." She laughed mirthlessly. "From what I have seen, its ghosts do not daunt her."

I touched the jewel Felipe had given me; it gave me strength. I said, "Supposing I tell you that I know Felipe has been in the habit of meeting his cousin. Supposing I also tell you that she's nothing to him but a—a scrap of the past."

Mary sighed. "You are being deluded, Ada," she said sadly. "The two of them are only using you, cruelly. I heard Pilar tell him to visit you—but it will be her he is coming to see. It is Pilar that he still loves devotedly. . . . I know, not three days since, they met at the House of Tears —and she told him that when the time was right, she would go to Mexico as they had planned."

"And what did he say?" I faltered.

"He smiled and kissed her."

"I don't believe it!" I cried. "You're lying."

"Do you think I could be so cruel, Ada?"

"He—he said he loved *me*. He made love to me. He . . . why . . ."

"It is not difficult to make love to a young eager girl who is too naive to hide her feelings." Mary put her hands over her face. "It . . . it's not difficult at all," she said in a muffled voice.

"But—if you heard him—today, you heard him talk about Pilar and the p-past . . ."

"You mentioned Pilar, Ada, and he was clever enough to make use of it."

"He promised me a ring—he gave me this." I trust the medallion at her.

"He only promised you a ring," Mary said. Her eyes darkened. "Promises are easy to make." She sighed. "If his intentions are honorable, why did he swear you to secrecy?"

"Because of Pilar!" I cried.

"Yes, because of Pilar," Mary agreed.

"It's over between them," I said defiantly. "I feel it."

"In three days?"

"Pilar is jealous of me. You saw it yourself!"

"She is playing a game, Ada. She is pretending to be jealous—and she will go on pretending—for your benefit, but from what I saw, she has no reason to be jealous. None at all!"

I felt cold—not flesh-cold but stone-cold, like a statue. I spoke in a statue's voice—with no inflections. I said, "Have you told Henry?"

"No."

"Shouldn't he know?"

Mary looked down. "I couldn't bring myself to do it," she whispered. "I am a guest in this house. I hoped against hope that it might come to nothing."

"I don't believe you," I said in that voice that did not seem to be coming from my lips. "I think you wanted it to happen, so then you could step in to comfort him as once you comforted my father—comforted and claimed him for yourself."

Her eyes were pain-filled. Tremulously, she said, "That wasn't the way of it. Your dear, good father . . ." Biting her lips, she looked at me hopelessly. "It would do no good to tell you what really happened, you—you'd only hate me the more. But I am your friend, Ada. You'll never have a better one. If there was only something I could do to prove how much I care for you. You see, once I was very like you, a little spoiled, but innocent, vulnerable, believing and— Oh, Ada, profit by my experience, please." She reached for my hand.

I thrust her away, "Why did you have to tell me so quickly! Couldn't you have let me be happy for just a day?"

"Would you have wanted your happiness to be founded on a lie?"

"It's not a lie! It's not!" I sobbed. "He loves me. You're jealous because you're all alone—in spite of your determined efforts to seduce my cousin!" I was not sure what "seduce" meant, but I had a feeling it was not a good word. Certainly it affected Mary adversely; springing to her feet, she ran out of the room, closing the door violently behind her.

My thoughts were chaotic. I did not want to believe Mary. She was lying, as usual—she had to be lying. Yet I had the uneasy conviction she was not. Furthermore, I recalled my own qualms about Don Felipe. Realistically speaking, it had seemed impossible for him to have fallen in love with me after only four meetings—he was no child, he was a man of the world, experienced and nearly thirty! He did not love me. I *had* been deceived—I and my Cousin Henry, too. Poor Henry. Mary might stand by and saying nothing, but I would not. I would tell him. I did not stop to think about consequences. I did not consider anything save my own hurt pride and betrayed love. I rushed out of my room and down into the patio. I slipped into the arbor, where I determined to wait until Henry came home.

Unfortunately, he did not come home—not while I waited in the arbor. The moon was high in the sky by the time I crawled stiffly out of it and made my way back to my room. Furiously, I went to bed, but not to sleep. I knew there was little chance of that; I would lie awake and contemplate my dead hopes and console myself with the dire things Henry might do, once he learned of his wife's deception. I had a wistful vision of Othello's towering madness, but I could not quite see Henry in the throes of such a passion. More likely he would . . . would . . . I fell asleep. When I awakened, it was morning.

The passage of nearly twelve hours did not affect my decision. It only changed the location. I would find some way of speaking to Henry in the corral or the fields or somewhere, anyhow. Grimly, I performed my ablutions, then I laced myself into my corset, drawing the strings so tightly I could hardly breathe. The stiffness lent me strength. I put on one of my black gowns and combed my hair back from my face, knotting it severely below my neck. A glance in the mirror should have showed me a face aged by sorrow and disappointment; instead I merely looked sulky. That same glance, however, showed me that I had forgotten to remove the medallion. I took it off and wrapped it among the folds of the green shawl. When I had the opportunity I would send them back to Don Felipe. Perhaps, I reasoned ironically, Pilar could take them to him. Except after I had spoken to Henry, she would probably not see Felipe any more.

The bell, summoning the household to early Mass, interrupted these vengeful thoughts. I hurried down to the chapel, intending to wait inside the door until Henry should either come in or out. Then, I . . .

He was not there! He was not on the veranda or in the patio, hall, parlor, dining room, ballroom, upstairs bedrooms, kitchen quarters. When I reached the corral, I learned he had ridden off in the early dawn in company with several other men. No one knew when he was coming back. More frustrated than ever, I went toward the house just as another bell was ringing—it was time for early breakfast.

Though the thought of sitting at table with Pilar and

Mary was singularly repugnant, I discovered that I was famished. Feeling much like Daniel in the lion's den, I took my place. Pilar gave me a solicitous smile. "My poor Ada," she said, "you look very wan. Have you not been well?"

I disregarded the impulse to throw the contents of my cup of chocolate in her face. "I had a slight upset," I said calmly. "Where is Henry?"

She shook her head. "He is with Mr. Larkin, his great friend."

"When are they going to fight?" Javier demanded.

Pilar gave him an exasperated look. "What is this talk of fighting?"

"But Mama, you know there's a plot to . . ."

"I know nothing of any plots." She frowned at Javier. "And nor do you. It is all rumor, and I am tired of it. Why does not Mr. Larkin attend to his own business, instead of putting his long Yankee fingers in matters that do not concern him?"

"What matters would those be?" Mary asked.

Pilar's eyes flashed. "Oh, we of Monterey all know Mr. Larkin is much more than the American consul here. We know that he wishes to bring California into his United States and rob the Dons of all their holdings. Look what has happened in Texas."

"And is your present government so satisfactory?" Mary asked softly.

"What do you know about our present government?" Pilar demanded insolently. "You have talked too much with my husband."

"I have never discussed your government with Henry. My father . . ."

"But you have discussed much else!" Pilar broke in. "Do not imagine I am unaware of your many discussions—of your meetings in hidden places. Do not imagine I am not aware of your guilty love. There have been many eyes to watch you, Señora Brett!"

Mary started up from the table. "And many mouths to lie!" she retorted. "I have had no secret meetings with your husband, though I imagine you'd like to believe I had, in order to—salve your own conscience." I looked at Mary amazed; I had never seen her so angry.

"Liar—little liar," Pilar hissed. "Unlike my husband, I

am not wound around your fingers. I am not a man to be deluded by your angel's face. I know what you are. . . ."

"Mama, Mama, do not speak so meanly to Señora Brett!" Javier cried shrilly. Running to Mary, he threw his arms around her. "I love her."

Mary gently loosed his clinging hands. "That is all right, Javier," she said, and then she left the room swiftly.

Pilar sprang to her feet. "That woman must and will leave my house," she intoned, flinging her arms out dramatically. "She has stolen both my husband and my son!"

In view of what I had been told about her relations with Don Felipe, I found her air of tragic betrayal ludicrous indeed. Since I was hard put to keep from laughing in her face, I murmured a hasty excuse and left the table.

As I came up on the balcony, I thought I heard the sound of muffled sobbing coming from Mary's chamber. In spite of my anger with her, I was tempted to try and comfort her, but as I neared her door, I hesitated. Could I tell her I did not believe Pilar? That would not be true, I decided suddenly. As I pondered on the altercation at the breakfast table, all my former suspicions were reactivated. Turning, I ran into my room and got out my diary, feverishly rereading all I had written during the voyage and in Valparaiso.

When at length I put it down, I was seething with fury. It all made sense—everything, even the way Henry had studiously avoided Mary since our arrival. Certainly, he would not want his poor betrayed wife to suspect them. And as for Pilar—no wonder she had turned to her cousin—and Felipe, naturally he had been sorry for her and . . .

"It is all Mary's fault," I wrote in my diary. "She has ruined my whole life!"

By the time I had finished writing what proved to be several pages of denunciation, it was close to ten in the morning and past the hour when I was accustomed to meet Javier and Rosa. I hurried downstairs, but I did not see the children anywhere. It was just as well, I thought. I was hardly in the mood to delve into the intricacies of English grammar!

Sinking down on a bench in the shady part of the veranda, I tried in vain to forget my own woes by admiring the beauty of the sunlit garden. I was unsuccessful. The sunshine, the plashing of the fountain, the insouciant chatter of the Indian girls, the darting humming birds, the buzzing bees, the brilliance of the trees and flowers, only served to oppress me. It was nearly October! Looking up at that serene cerulean sky, I silently accused it of duplicity. October ought to look like October! I wanted to go home—that was what I wanted! In Concord, I should have been able to wear my medium-weight woolen shawl over a merino dress, I would not be feeling so intensely warm. I would go home, I decided. Yes, even though it meant another sea voyage and a stop in quaking Chile, I would leave as soon as I could make the necessary arrangements. I would settle in Concord or Boston and become a teacher or a writer. I would write about California. I would warn . . .

"Señorita." A quavering voice dispersed my thoughts. I looked up to find the elderly peon Hueso standing in front of me. Don Felipe's servant!

A pulse began to beat in my throat. I had to speak over it. I said, "Yes?"

"I am sent for you, señorita. You must come with me," he said.

"Come with you—why?" I faltered, feeling frightened.

"Don Felipe is very sick . . . very, very sick." The peon shook his head. "He is asking for you."

"Sick? What is the matter with him?"

The old man looked vague. "They do not know, señorita. . . . It is his head, they think. He grew dizzy and fell from his horse . . . he is badly hurt . . . a priest has been summoned . . . but also, he asks for you, señorita. Often he asks . . ."

I forgot that I had ever been angry. "Where is he?" I jumped to my feet. "Quick, take me to him!"

"They have brought him to the house in the pine grove, señorita."

"The House of Tears!" I cried in horror. "Oh, God, will he die there, too?"

The peon shook his head. "I do not know, señorita. I know only that he asks for you and that they said I must fetch you. . . ."

Dazedly, I followed him out of the patio. It was only when we were halfway across the fields that it occurred to me that I had told no one of my destination, but that thought was soon engulfed by my greater fear and I continued on my way, inwardly decrying the fact that I had not come by horseback—old Hueso walked so very slowly.

However, at last we were in sight of that ruined wall and the tangled garden. "Where is he?" I cried to Hueso. "Where shall I go?"

Hueso looked at me vaguely. "In there, señorita," he mumbled, pointing to the garden.

I ran toward the wall and clambered over it, dropping to my knees amidst a thorny tangle of plants and flowers. As I struggled to my feet, I heard a sound that chilled my blood! A hollow clang!

Looking up, I saw the bell of the tower slowly swinging back and forth in its crumbling niche. I could not blame the wind. There was no wind. As I shrank back, fearfully, I had a second, even greater shock—from around that remnant of wall stepped a cowled figure. I gazed at it in horror. Was I being confronted by the spirit of damned Father Anselmo? No, a second glance assured me that I was looking at substance, for a shadow had been cast across the path. Hueso had told me a priest had been summoned.

"You—you are here for Don Felipe?" I hazarded.

The monk nodded. "I am here to save his soul."

"He—he's still alive—isn't he?" I cried. "Oh, please, take me to him."

The monk made no move to obey. Statue-still, he stood facing me. "He is still alive—and it is to be hoped that his senses will soon be restored."

"He's unconscious!"

"Unconscious, yes—of many things, señorita. He is unconscious of his obligations to his family and to his country. He might have avenged the wrongs that were done us, but he is strangely reluctant—and for that, we can blame only you!"

I hate to admit it, but at that moment my mouth fell open, just the way it is supposed to do in novels. Naturally, in such a position, I was bereft of words. Even if I had been able to speak, I am sure I could have found nothing to say, not even when the man in front of me threw back his cowl to reveal the sleek black head and the all-too-familiar features of Don Cruz de Silva. He gave me a mocking smile. "No doubt you are wondering what I am doing here, why I am dressed in this deceptive manner, and what it all means?" He frowned. "You will find out, señorita, before you are much older. Please, come with me." He reached for my arm.

I whirled back. "What do you want with me?" I demanded furiously. "Why was I . . . ?"

"No questions, please!" he ordered. "I have promised you may have all the answers you need, but not at this precise moment. At this moment . . ."

Though I did not know why I was in danger, there was something so menacing in his attitude, and the expression in his narrowed eyes was so repellent, that I turned and ran in the direction I had come.

"Run, run little mouse," he called after me. "Give our cats some exercise!"

I knew that my action was futile, but desperately I made for the gate and flung myself against it. Yet even as I reached it, I felt a hand on my arm. "Let me go!" I cried desperately.

"Ada!"

I looked—and looked a second time at my captor. "Mary!" I whispered.

She was pale and breathing hard, as if she too had been running. She did not relinquish her hold. "Ada, dear," she said urgently. "Listen to me . . . Oh God!" She stiffened as she looked over my shoulder.

I looked too, and saw them—a horde of black-robed figures. Some wore cowls but others were bareheaded, and though their garb proclaimed them monks, I could see even in that first cursory glance that they had no more right to the habit than did Don Cruz. Indeed, with their cropped ears, their marked faces and brutal expressions, they bore a horrid resemblance to the men we had encountered on the road. Don Cruz strolled up to us and put his hand on Mary's shoulder.

"A most fortuitous meeting," he said softly. "Two for the price of one and a chance to do my Cousin Pilar yet another favor."

"Your—Cousin Pilar . . .?"

He nodded. "My poor little cousin who is so unhappy . . . who has been bereft of all love . . . who has only misery and hate in her heart. Oh, how she does hate the two of you—it is a passion that consumes her. . . ."

"What do you want with us?" Mary demanded.

"I want you and your countrymen to leave us in peace,"

he said sharply. "And since persuasion will accomplish nothing, we must use other more forceful methods. Tonight you and all the Americans in this peninsula will be taking a journey—a long journey to beautiful Mexico."

With a shudder, I remembered the Alvarado incident. "You would put us in prison?" I asked, numbly.

"In prison," he echoed, laughing. "But of course not, señorita. That would serve no purpose. My plans for you —and for your lovely stepmother—are quite, quite different—and certainly more profitable."

"You mean to hold us for ransom!" I exclaimed.

"For ransom?" He continued to laugh. "Oh, no, I am far more imaginative than that, señorita. The profit I would turn will be much greater than a single ransom payment. . . ."

Mary put her arms around me protectively. "It will not happen!" she cried. "What you have in mind—it will not happen."

Don Cruz's eyes narrowed. "I see you understand, señora. You are indeed a woman of the world, are you not? And this little one will quickly cease to pine for my brother, for soon she will have all the lovers she wants. One for each of her waking hours—or working hours—. It is all the same, is it not?"

His words would have been completely obscure to me had I not seen Mary's reaction. Her eyes were filled with horror and she had grown very pale, but she still said firmly, "I tell you it will not happen. Something—someone— will stop you. And all this misery you hope to inflict on us will instead be visited upon you!"

Don Cruz's smile disappeared. "Am I to understand that you are cursing me, Señora Brett?"

"Yes," she said in a strange voice. "I do curse you. With the powers that I have been given, I curse you."

Looking at her pale set face, I shuddered. It seemed to me that Mary had become a stranger, a stranger to be feared. Don Cruz appeared to have been similarly affected, for he turned away quickly. I heard the men mutter among themselves, and one of them cried out: "She does have the evil eye. . . ."

"Be silent," Don Cruz said furiously. "She does not have the evil eye. That is nothing but a childish superstition. As for her curses, I do not fear them. I fear only guns and swords, and so should you!"

"Libardo said, before he went to his death, that . . ." a man started to say.

"Libardo was careless," rasped Don Cruz; "she caught him off-guard, that's how she escaped him. Words and looks cannot destroy you, I tell you—but carelessness can."

I looked at him in shock. "It—it was you that day. Your men, not the soldiers of Micheltorena . . ." I said.

"Yes, señorita." He nodded. "My own men . . ."

"But your brother was hurt!"

His eyes blazed. "That was an accident, a most regrettable accident. I assure you that the men responsible for it were reprimanded."

"Your brother knew that . . . that you . . ."

His smile returned. "Yes, Señorita Ada, he knew—and he has accepted my apology. But now we have no more time to pass in pleasant conversation. We must be on our way. Juan!" He signaled one of his men. "Bind their wrists. Attend first to the señora."

The man he had summoned came forward reluctantly, eyeing Mary with awe; but he produced a stout cord, and grasping her arms, he pulled them behind her, lashing her wrists together. Cruz watched the procedure closely.

"Make the knots tighter," he ordered. "The devil has nimble fingers and if he should aid the señora . . ."

"Cruz . . . Cousin Cruz . . ." A shrill, indignant cry startled us all as Javier suddenly sprang into our midst. The man who had been holding Mary's wrists backed away, his eyes wide with fear.

"Come!" Don Cruz snapped. "It is not the devil, Juan. It is only little Javier, being mischievous." With an effort, he smiled down at the boy. "What has brought you here?"

"I followed the Señora Maria," Javier said. "Often I have seen her go to the pine grove and today I thought I would discover why. I am too old to be afraid of ghosts, I think. But why . . ."

"Oh, Javier . . . Javier . . ." Mary sighed. "That was very foolish. . . ."

"Now that you are here, you may go home—and immediately," Don Cruz rasped.

"I shan't. You are hurting the Señora Maria. Why are you hurting her?"

"This is not your concern, Javier!" Cruz said coldly.

Javier glared up at him. "You must not hurt her. She is good and kind."

"She is an American," Cruz said. "Have you forgotten that? And unless we rid ourselves of this plague of locusts, our lands will be forfeit and our people destitute. Is that what you want, Javier?"

Confusion was written large on the child's face. He looked from his cousin to Mary, then he ran to her. "Even if she is an American, I love her!" he cried. "I shall not let you hurt her! Release her at once!"

Don Cruz's eyes narrowed and the grimace that showed his teeth was the merest travesty of a smile. "So be it. You have chosen."

His expression terrified me. "He—he is only a child," I said.

"When soldiers put a town to the sword, they do not spare the children because they know that from the seed will grow the tree," Don Cruz said.

Suddenly, Javier picked up a handful of dirt and flung it at Don Cruz. "Let the Señora Maria go!" he cried again.

A chorus of guttural laughter greeted his action, but a look from Don Cruz was enough to sile ce his men. He turned on Mary. "This is your devil, no do bt, Señora Brett —well, we will bring him with us. That shou d please you."

Mary expelled a long quivering breath. 'He is Pilar's child, too—she would be frantic. . . ."

"It is not too late for my cousin to have other sons— strong sons with blood that is undiluted by the American strain."

My knees grew weak. "You—you'd not send Javier— with—with the others—"

"As you saw, señorita, he has made his choice, and since he is a half-breed . . ."

"I'm not! I'm not! I'm a Californio!" Javier screamed.

"Don Cruz," a man muttered. "It grows late."

"You are right to remind me." Don Cruz nodded. "Yes, it grows late, and if we are to reach our destination by mid-afternoon, we must hurry. Well, Javier, you have always wished to come to my camp in the mountains, and to-day you shall."

Javier looked at him uncertainly. "I don't think I want to go with you, Cousin Cruz."

Don Cruz scooped the child up in his arms. "Your wishes are no longer my concern," he said, tossing the boy to one of his men. "Bind him."

I was pleased to see that the order was not effected as quickly as Don Cruz might have wished, for Javier wriggled, kicked, and bit, the while he shrilled, "My father will punish you for this—he will!"

"Your father will be on the way to Mexico with the rest of your accursed race," Don Cruz told him coldly. "As he should have been long ago if Don Hilario had listened to me." He glared down at the ground. "Do you see the pass to which you have brought us, Uncle Hilario—do you see it from the hell to which I sent you?"

I grew cold. "Oh, God!" I cried. "Henry was right. He was murdered!"

Don Cruz whirled on me. "He was not murdered, señorita, he was executed—as all traitors must be and will be before this day is at an end."

"You are mad!" I exclaimed.

"If it is madness to love my homeland, then I must agree with you, señorita, and I will tell you, too, that I am glad I am afflicted with such a madness!" Turning to his men, he snapped an order: "Secure the prisoners and let us be going!"

In practically that same instant, I was seized from behind, my wrists were tightly bound, and a most uncomfortable wad of cloth was thrust into my mouth and held there by a filthy red bandanna that smelled most vilely of aged tobacco and sweat. I was pushed down on the ground and left there beside Mary and Javier, who had sustained similar treatment.

Hopelessly, Mary and I looked at each other, but though we were both frightened, I knew that she as much as I was more concerned over Javier's plight. Not only was he in danger, but he had suffered a cruel disappointment in the hands of the cousin he had adored. Yet there was no fear in his eyes; there was only anger, and a grimness I had never seen before. It hurt me—he was far too young to experience such adult emotions, far too young to have had his trust destroyed. It was then that I knew beyond all doubt that I had never really hated anyone—no, not even Mary Booth—because I had lately learned what it actually meant to hate, and ironically, Don Cruz de Silva, the brother of the man I had thought I loved, had been my teacher.

We were bestowed in a large carreta. The canvas curtains of the vehicle were drawn so tightly that no light could penetrate, but if the sun was banished, its heat remained; it was nearly stifling! Even though my dress was thin silk, its folds were heavy and clinging, and there was also the gag in my mouth, pressing against my tongue. Though I tried to relieve this pressure by biting down on the cloth, it was a horrible feeling. Yet if my physical discomfort was great, it was exceeded by my mental misery, for I could not help blaming myself for everything that had happened. I was literally deluged with 'ifs."

If I had not fallen in love with Felipe, so suddenly and so completely. If I had only listened to Mary when she told me of his perfidy—but I had listened, and then Hueso had come with his lies. The litany of "ifs" began again. If only I had not heeded Hueso. If only I had hardened my heart against Felipe. If only I hadn't gone with Hueso. If . . . And where was Felipe? Did he know what happened to us? Had he helped plan our kidnapping? He had known about the assault on the road. I frowned. That was very confusing; if he had known, why . . . ? I abandoned that particular trail of thought—it led me into a cul-de-sac. Certainly, Felipe must know of Don Cruz's present plans—or did he? I thought of Don Cruz's reasons for kidnapping me. He had said that I had turned Felipe's mind from his obligations. If I had done that, then perhaps he really did care for me. Perhaps . . . My self-searching ended abruptly. The cart must have been going up a steep hill, for all of us were roughly jumbled together, and now my physical discomfort did supersede my mental anguish!

The ride had seemed endless, but inevitably, the cart halted and we were lifted out and deposited on the ground. As my eyes grew accustomed to the daylight again, I saw that we were in a gorge so narrow that the cliffs on either side of it leaned toward us so menacingly that it seemed the slightest movement might send them tumbling down upon us. As I looked on that desolate landscape, I grew more frightened, for who would ever find us? I grimaced wryly —unknown to myself, I had actually been entertaining a hope of eventual rescue; yet even as I became aware of it, it vanished. Don Cruz could do with us what he wished, and no one would ever be the wiser. Against my will, the tears ran out of my eyes, and since I could not wipe them away, they remained for Don Cruz to see and ridicule when at last he came to stand over me.

He did not waste his opportunity. "You are frightened," he said with satisfaction. "And this is but the beginning of your ordeal, little Señorita Ada. There will come a time when you pray that your sufferings be ended, even by death —but you are young and strong, and death will not come to you so easily. You will live to see your beauty fade and disease rot the flesh from your bones. And when you finally die, they will throw your body into a pit outside the city gates and sprinkle it with quicklime. Then, my sweet, may your unhallowed spirit go wailing through the long Mexican nights." His laughter was as mad as his words. If I had been able to cover my ears, I should have, but my hands were still tied. I had to listen until at last that laughter was stilled—until he said softly, "But I hope you will not blame me for your woes, señorita—or curse me as your stepmother has done, for which she will pay. If you have curses, lay them on the head of your thieving Cousin Enrico, whose actions you shall soon interpret for us. Take her inside!"

One of his men lifted me in his arms and carried me through a clump of trees to an adobe house. Beside its rude doorway was an immense cage, which housed a restless grizzly bear. As we approached, it rose on its hind legs, snarling ferociously. I felt my captor tremble, but Don Cruz, albeit he stood some three feet from the cage, raised his hand in a salute.

"Hail, Doña Dolores," he said softly. "Is she not beautiful? She is very brave. She put up a great fight against me, but I won. She will fight well, too, when she is chained to the bull in the arena. Perhaps then she will win. Either way, I shall have her skin, and I shall treasure it in memory of the one woman I have been able to admire."

Fearful as she was, I felt a certain kinship with the mighty beast—were we not both the victims of Don Cruz de Silva? Her sudden snarl and snap I took for tacit agreement.

The interior of the house was rough—the beams stretching across its ceiling unfinished, the walls only imperfectly plastered, the floor of beaten mud. I was taken through several rooms of varying size and deposited in the last of these, a tiny, cell-like chamber furnished with a chair and a cot of rawhide stretched over a wooden frame. A single small window was heavily barred. My captor pushed me inside so roughly that I lost my balance and fell heavily. Before I could scramble to my feet, two Indian women had entered. Both were massively built. Their dark features registered neither pity nor concern. Quickly and quietly, they pulled me to my feet, freed my numbed hands and removed the gag from my mouth. Then, as silently as they had come, they left, and I heard a chain being pulled across the door.

Naturally, as soon as circulation was restored, I made all those futile efforts common to any prisoner. I tried the door, but of course it did not yield; the bars on the windows remained regrettably firm, and I did not have much of a view beyond them. I saw only the dense greenery of some massed firs. Meanwhile, because sensation had returned to my benumbed arms and hands and because my tongue was allowed free play in its domain, I became aware of those other discomforts kept in abeyance during my greater agony. I was thirsty, hungry, hot, dirty. My hair was filled with dust and matted with perspiration. In all, I was in a deplorable state. And why? Because I was an American, an interloper in this sequestered paradise. Was that my sole crime? I could think of nothing else—then, inside my head, I heard the flapping of great wings, the raucous bray of the bird they called the albatross. Months ago, I had witnessed the shooting of those unwieldy creatures, and now, it seemed, all seven of them had been hung about my neck. I was startled by my own laughter.

"Ridiculous!" I said. But a moment later, I had decided that it was as reasonable an explanation as any.

I had expected Don Cruz to return immediately, and for a good quarter hour, I paced up and down, bracing myself for the threatened ordeal; but he did not appear. Finally, I lay down on the narrow cot. As usual, the last thing I expected to do was sleep, and as usual, it was the first thing that happened to me. I fell into a sleep so deep and dreamless that when I finally awakened I had lost all sense of time and place. I stared blankly at the rough walls of my chamber, trying to locate the familiar pieces of furniture in my bedroom, and it was only when I saw the iron bars on the window that I became fully aware of my plight. I sat up shakily, wondering how long I had slept. The bar-bisected square before me had grown dimmer, and when I went to it, I saw the moon brightening against the dark blue sky. It was nearly evening. Why had I been left undisturbed so long? What had happened to my companions? Recalling a novel I had once read about prisoners in a dungeon, I went to the wall and tapped experimentally against it, hoping to hear a distant answering thud; then I remembered that adobe walls were at least four feet thick. Returning to my cot, I lay down again. More time passed, and nearly all the light had gone, before I heard footsteps in the passage outside my door. Tensing, I sat up. As the chain rattled, I made a silent vow: *I will not cry out nor weep. No matter what happens to me, Don Cruz will see no tears!*

As my door opened, I blinked against the sudden brightness of an oil lamp and heard Don Cruz say contemptuously, "Here she is."

"My dear Cruz, I fail to see why you thought it necessary to bring her here."

At the sound of that voice, my heart pounded so heavily I wondered it was not audible. "Don Felipe," I whispered.

He stepped into the room, and by the light of the lamp he carried, I saw the face of a man I had once met on the way to my cousin's house—cold, proud, arrogant. He gave me no more than a cursory glance before he turned to Don Cruz. "Surely you did not imagine I had any real interest in this child?" he inquired haughtily.

"Pilar seemed to think differently—also my men informed me of your meetings. . . ."

Don Felipe's laugh was light. "I have often given you my opinion of your rogues, my dear Cruz. They failed to stop Enrico in Boston, they failed on shipboard, then there was that most unfortunate episode on the road—in which I nearly lost my life. And now they have failed again."

I turned cold, thinking of Henry's fall in Boston, that moment when our Spanish passenger lost his footing and nearly thrust my cousin overboard, and . . . But I had no time for memories—Don Cruz was speaking again. He said, "They did not fail to describe your ardent pursuit . . ."

"Please." Don Felipe laughed again. "She was only a means to an end, Cruz. With Enrico home, it was more and more difficult to meet Pilar. If I could have become the accepted suitor of this most willing little girl . . ."

"Pilar thought . . ." Cruz interrupted.

"I do not understand Pilar," Felipe sighed. "For ten

years she has had all my devotion, yet she distrusts and doubts me. And you, my own brother, knowing my sentiments, knowing how I have suffered over her—would I be likely to turn in a week's time to a relation of Enrico Slade?"

"I have been of two minds about your sentiments, Felipe. We've had little to say to each other since your—accident. Where have you been during the last days? What have you been doing? You would not go with me to our meetings. Indeed, you said you would not be involved in these petty intrigues. You called it a madness. . . ."

"And still I call it so," Don Felipe retorted. "Still I think you have not made your plans carefully enough, still I think you are being too hasty. How can you be sure that you will have all the support you need?"

"I am sure," Don Cruz said. "They will not fail me. They are not my only brother!"

The lantern quivered in Don Felipe's grasp and the light jumped crazily over the walls. "You've no right to say that!" he exclaimed. "I have not failed you!"

"Nor have you helped me, Felipe."

"But I have come to help you, Cruz," Don Felipe said vehemently.

Don Cruz's voice was doubtful. "Is that why you came?"

"What other reason would I have? When Pilar told me your plans, I'd no other thought than to join you."

"No other thought? What about the Señorita Ada?"

"I have told you my reasons for that."

"And you swear they are the truth?"

"On the head of our sainted mother, on the head of the Lord Jesus Christ, I swear that I have come to help you, Cruz," Don Felipe said solemnly; and listening to that oath, my heart sank, because I knew that he *had* to be telling the truth.

There was a moment's pause, and then in a voice choked with emotion, Don Cruz said, "My brother, you have come to your senses at last. It is your country that matters, after all."

"I have come to my senses. It is my country that matters," Don Felipe agreed.

"Tonight, when our other commanders arrive, we will ride together!" Don Cruz exclaimed joyfully.

"When do you expect them?" Don Felipe demanded.

"Within the hour," Don Cruz said complacently. "By

noon tomorrow, there will not be one American dog left in all of Monterey, and when those in the other cities learn what we have accomplished, they will follow our example. All the foreigners will go—men, women, children!"

I suddenly found my voice. *"Olé!"* I mocked, and clapped my hands. "It is a brave man indeed who makes war on men, women, and little children, including his own cousin. Do you know why Javier learned English, Don Cruz? So that he might spy for you. He was your greatest ally—your greatest defender. He loved you with all his heart!"

"Javier!" Don Felipe turned to Cruz. "What is this about Javier?"

A wild hope surged through me. Don Felipe had not been told of Javier's presence in the camp. Might it enrage him or arouse a lingering sense of decency? All evidence to the contrary, I could not believe him the fanatic his brother was. I cried out: "Javier is here because he has tainted blood, and that makes him a traitor like his late grandfather, Don Hilario. All traitors must die!"

"Die? Javier?" Don Felipe asked incredulously.

"He will not die," Cruz said sharply. "He will be sent to Mexico with the others. Let Pilar give you sons who have the right to inherit the broad acres of the Villeneuvas."

Don Felipe's eyes had narrowed. "What did she mean about Don Hilario?" he asked.

Don Cruz hesitated, but I said, "You don't know how Don Hilario died?"

Don Felipe kept his eyes on his brother. "It was an accident, I was told. A fall from his horse."

"I was told it was an execution," I said.

"An execution . . . ?" Don Felipe repeated.

"In the name of patriotism!" I cried contemptuously.

Don Felipe shook his head. "You killed our uncle, Cruz?"

"He signed his own death warrant," Cruz said excitedly. "He signed it when he bade his only daughter marry the American and when he deeded the lands of the Villeneuvas to that same damned American. It was a double crime—against his family, against his people. If I could have killed him twice, I should have been the happier!"

"Madre de Dios!" Don Felipe said in a low voice.

"Will you chide me for it, then? I did it for you. I did it for our country. You must believe that!"

My heart sank as Don Felipe nodded. "Yes, I do believe it."

With a long sigh, Don Cruz embraced him. "My brother," he said emotionally. "My brother in blood, my brother of the spirit. Together we will be invincible!"

"Yes, invincible!" Don Felipe cried in ringing tones. A thousand protests, a thousand denunciations, struggled for expression, but I kept my lips shut against them and merely listened as Don Felipe continued: "Will your prisoners be brought here?"

Don Cruz shook his head. "We've not the facilities or the space. It is a pity we could not involve Micheltorena, for then we might have used the jail, as before—but, still, we've no cause for complaint. Don Manuel Ortega has—loaned—us his barn. It is strongly built and not conspicuous from the road."

Don Felipe smiled. "I did not know Don Manuel was of our number."

"There are many you do not know, Felipe." Cruz smiled. "But you will know them soon." He turned to me. "Indeed, it is to be hoped that we will both garner much knowledge before the night is over. I, for instance, wish to hear about the activities of Enrico Slade—from the time he returned to his homeland last year to this present moment. Perhaps Señorita Ada will be so kind as to tell us?"

"Yes," Don Felipe agreed; "that would be most enlightening."

I looked at them with disbelief. "I—I don't understand you," I stuttered.

"Do you not?" Don Cruz came close to me. "I've the feeling you do, señorita. I have the feeling you know exactly why Enrico went to Washington, and what was said during his audience with the Secretary of War."

Blankly, I said, "I can't imagine what you're talking about."

He struck me violently across the face. "Let me prod your memory, señorita!"

I scarcely felt the blow. My eyes were on Don Felipe. Incredibly, he was smiling. He said gently, "Best tell my brother what he wishes to know, señorita."

Contemptuously, I faced Cruz. "I don't know anything, and if I did, I should never tell you!"

Don Cruz shook me. "Liar, little liar!" he hissed.

"Cruz," Don Felipe frowned. "Let her alone."

"You defend her?" Don Cruz released me abruptly and turned on his brother.

Don Felipe shook his head, "Not at all. There are better ways to coerce her—such as a whip." Moving to me, he seized my arm in a grip so hard it sent little arrows of pain coursing up to my shoulder. "We will leave you for the present, my little stubborn señorita, and when we return, we shall bring with us a strong rawhide whip, of the sort that cuts the skin of the bark into small pieces. Would you do us the favor of talking now—or will you wait?"

I spat in his face.

Furiously, he seized me in his arms, shaking me violently, and then he released me so quickly that I fell off the cot and onto the floor. Drawing his sleeve across his mouth, he wiped away the spittle, saying, "We will return soon, señorita."

Don Cruz added, "And I advise you to loosen you tongue—otherwise, we will loosen your flesh."

Even after they had gone, I still lay where I had fallen. I did not cry. My anger was of the hot, burning sort that must needs dry the tear-wells. Though danger and pain were imminent, I could not concentrate on these; I could only think of Don Felipe and remember that the man who had spoken so tauntingly and who had treated me so cruelly had once held me in his arms and sworn he loved me. Why? I had heard the reason from both his and Mary's lips —so that he could see his cousin without arousing Henry's suspicions. But he needn't have made love to me. He could have courted me with those empty attentions I had received from the other caballeros. Why had he found it necessary to . . . In the midst of my agonized theorizing, I heard three shots! I stiffened, wondering what they might presage. An attack on the camp? From the camp?

I ran to the window, but of course I could see nothing through the darkened mass of trees. But I *heard* something —a muffled sound, which at first I could not identify. As I strained to listen, it grew louder and closer. Horses' hooves, that's what it was. Were Cruz's men arriving? I had not thought they would come so soon, but he had said within the hour. The noise increased, and I shuddered, for it suggested to me a huge band of men, an army to fall upon us and uproot the Larkins, the Slades, and every other ill-advised foreigner who had ever thought to settle here. And what dark fate lay in store for Mary and myself? Suddenly, I could think no longer. My ears were battered by the sound of yelling and, incredibly, of gunfire—but why would they be shooting at their own men and why—? Horses neighed wildly and somewhere a woman screamed. Mary? The agonized yell of a man in pain reached me. Gripping the bars of my window, I tried to interpret what I was hearing. It was a battle, it had to be a battle, and it must have been caused by a surprise attack—but from whom, and who would emerge victorious?

Once again I heard footsteps in the passageway, then a chain dropped to the floor and my door was pulled open by a man who rushed into my room and seized me in his arms. I struggled fiercely, trying to bite and scratch, but I was no match for him. Pinioning my arms to my sides, he held me fast. "Ada . . . Ada . . ." he whispered urgently. "I have come to help you, my love. It is all over. My brother's men are outnumbered—already they have surrendered. You are safe."

I continued to struggle. "Let me go," I cried. "I don't believe you . . . you are trying to save yourself. But I shall tell them what you are . . . I shall tell . . ."

"My brave, my lovely Ada!" He laughed. "They will tell you what I am, and how I gave them the signal to attack. They will tell you also that I had to frighten you—it was all part of the plan to throw my poor misguided brother off-guard." He sighed. "Always I knew he was wild, but I never knew that he was insane. . . . And to think that he would have taken you . . . my beautiful, my heart." He kissed me, not once but many times, and when at length he raised his head, I threw my arms around his neck and would not let him go. I do not know how long we stood there, pressed against each other, but I know that in those moments, part of me went into his keeping. I knew, too, that I would never be a whole person again—I would not want to be.

Finally, reluctantly, he moved away from me. "Come, love, I will see that you are taken home."

"I want to be with you," I whispered.

"I want to keep you with me—as long as we both shall live," he said, caressing me. "But not tonight, when there are still more dangers to be faced. Come."

We came forth from that house into chaos. All around me in the clearing, men were groaning, shouting, and cursing; others were horribly still and silent. I saw, illumined by a campfire, a band of soldiers, their rifles trained on the corral where a small group of men, still in their monks' habits, crouched.

"Ada . . . Ada . . . are you all right?" Henry, a rifle slung over his shoulder, hurried up to me.

"You? Why . . ." I looked at him uncomprehendingly.

"Ada!" Mary hastened to me. "You're safe. I was so frightened for you." She put her arms around me.

"Oh, Mary—thank God, you're safe, too. Oh, Mary, I am so sorry—and Javier, where is Javier? I'm to blame for everything . . . I . . ." I started to cry.

"Don't, Ada."

"Let her cry," Felipe said. "She has every right to cry. "She has been too brave—far too brave." He looked at Henry. "And Enrico, you must tell her I am not a villain. . . ."

"He needs to tell me nothing!" I cried. "I believe you. But oh, Mary, where is Javier?"

"He's with his mother," she said gently.

My confusion increased. "With Pilar?"

"Yes, it is my cousin Pilar whom we must thank for all that has happened. It was she who gave the warning. . . ."

"But what has happened? How . . . ?"

"It is a long story, love, and one we've not the time to give you now. But later . . . after we have visited the Ortega barn . . ."

"Your brother!" I clutched his arm. "What happened to Don Cruz?"

He stiffened. "He was wounded in the first volley. I saw him fall. I have not yet been able to find his—him. I shall look once more before I go, but meanwhile—are you able to ride?"

Confusedly, I nodded yes. "But why . . . ?"

"Enrico will send men to take you home."

"But I was going to ask . . ."

He put his two fingers gently across my lips. "No questions, love, until I have time to tell you all." Putting his arm around me, he started to lead me across the clearing.

Suddenly, Mary screamed. "Ada, Ada, look out . . . Felipe . . ."

I was aware of a dark shape in front of me, rising from the ground, a pistol clutched in its hand—a face distorted with pain and rage. Even as I recognized Don Cruz, Mary leaped in front of me, and simultaneously a shot rang out and close by my ear another pistol returned the fire and Don Felipe cried out "Cruz, Cruz!" He ran to a fallen man, he lifted him in his arms, he said brokenly, "I had to do it . . . I had to do it . . ."

Meanwhile, I was staring uncomprehendingly at Mary, who lay on the ground at my feet, her golden hair in the dust, her face milk-white. Because her dress was the black of widowhood, I did not know until I knelt beside her that it was stained with scarlet. I screamed and screamed again —"Mary, Mary, Mary"—and lifted my reddened palm and screamed again.

"Maria!" my cries were hoarsely echoed. Amazingly, Señora Mendoza knelt beside me, smoothing Mary's tangled hair and murmuring little endearments.

Henry and Felipe brought her into the house, into a huge room which had evidently served as Don Cruz's working and living quarters. They put her on a rawhide cot and Señora Mendoza tore open her bodice, baring the ugly wound on her breast.

"We must have a doctor . . . a doctor . . ." someone repeated monotonously. For a moment, I did not realize that it was I who spoke.

"A doctor could not help her," Señora Mendoza said. "It is too late."

"She—she's not dead?" Henry groaned.

"Not yet. . . ." Señora Mendoza shook her head, her gray eyes somber, her mouth grim.

"Maria . . . Maria . . ." Pilar sank weeping onto a chair near the cot. Beside her, Javier sobbed quietly.

"Ada . . ." Mary's eyes opened. "Ada . . ." she gasped.

I stumbled forward to kneel at her side. "Mary . . ." I whispered, taking her hand.

Her expression was anxious. "You are safe?" she asked.

"Quite safe, Mary. But why . . . why did you do it?" I could say no more.

She smiled at me. "It's all right, my dear," she said softly. "I am not in any pain, you know. I feel nothing. . . . Where . . . is Felipe . . . ?"

"I am here, Maria," he said, coming to stand beside me. She sighed. "I misjudged you. . . ."

"I understand," he said. "It is all right, my Maria. . . ."

"But . . ." she began.

"Mary, you mustn't try to talk," Henry said. "Later . . ."

She moved her head slightly. "There will be no later, Henry."

"Mary, you . . . won't die. . . ." I wept.

"Oh, yes . . ." She nodded. "I am not afraid . . . anymore. . . . Señora Mendoza has taught me not to be afraid. . . . She has showed me . . . much . . . You see . . . I have expected death for a long time . . . ever since I looked across a hall in Boston . . . and saw my image . . . mirror-clear. You did not believe me, Henry . . . but it happened. . . . My old nurse told me about such things. . . ." She looked toward Señora Mendoza and smiled faintly. "Thank you, señora . . . for helping me. . . ."

"It is God who has helped you, Maria . . . who wanted you to see . . ." The granite face was curiously softened, the gray eyes full of love. I hardly recognized her.

"Am I forgiven, then. . . ?" Mary closed her eyes.

"Mary . . ." I wailed. "Is she . . . ?"

"No," she said faintly. With an effort, she looked at me. "I am growing very sleepy, Ada . . . but I—want you to know I—loved your father, very much. He saved my life. . . . I should have ended it with my own hand, I was in such despair, but he rescued me from evil. I loved him . . . I felt so safe with him . . . so safe . . ." She paused. "Henry must tell you everything . . . Henry . . ."

"Mary." He knelt beside me, his hand on her hair. "Mary, my dear," he said huskily.

"My dear friend . . . thank you for all you did for me." Her eyes widened suddenly and she looked beyond him. "Why . . . why, Arthur!" she exclaimed in delighted tones. "You . . . you are here, too?" Smiling, she stretched out her arms. "Oh, yes—I will!" she cried gladly. "Now!" And still smiling, she fell back dead.

A month later, I wrote the rest of Mary's story and my

own. I wrote of the raid on the Ortega ranch and the round-up of the conspirators, as well as of several captive Americans.

I wrote down all I had learned of Don Cruz's mad efforts to reactivate the old romance between his brother and his cousin Pilar, lonely in her husband's absence and not at all unwilling to flirt with the lover of her early youth. These smouldering cinders had been further kindled by Cruz's lies to Pilar concerning the shipboard romance of Mary and her husband, dutifully confided to him, he said, by a certain Spanish passenger. According to Cruz, Pilar stood to lose both her husband and her erstwhile lover to the Americans. Unhappy and insecure, she had agreed to my removal—that is, she had agreed until she had learned of Javier's kidnapping. Her informant had been none other than Señora Mendoza, who from her special eyrie in the House of Tears had watched and told, turning Pilar into a vengeful tigress determined to save her cub. She had then enlisted the unlikely combination of her husband and Don Felipe de Silva, whose smouldering anger at his brother's action burst into flame. He had long decried Cruz's fanaticism; he had also deplored the disorganization of California's government. A sane, well-traveled, far-seeing man, he had finally been able to swallow his old bitternesses and to see the advantages that might come with the statehood for which Cousin Henry, his immediate superior, Thomas Larkin, and their cohort, Charles Collier, were working—or plotting, if you like. He had hoped to convince his brother of the futility of fighting the inevitable. He had also hoped to ease himself out of a situation he had thought intolerable even before he met me. He had not minded indulging in a light flirtation with his Cousin Pilar, but the thought of marrying her had never occurred to him. Unlike Don Cruz, he had not cast covetous eyes on the Villenueva lands. Yet he, too, had received a dose of Cruz's poison and suspected Mary and Henry of a guilty attachment, a state of affairs that had aroused both his chivalry and his resentment, making it the more difficult for him to extricate himself from his involvement with Pilar. I could not fault him for believing Don Cruz. Had I not arrived at much the same conclusion even without the benefit of his insinuations?

As I set down Mary's pitiable story, my sense of shame was so great I could scarcely write; but I persevered. From

Henry and from Señora Mendoza, I pieced the tale together —the tale of a naïve young girl raised by a superstitious nurse who not only filled her mind with tales of wonder, but who was, in effect, a practicing witch—if you can believe such people exist in this year of 1843! She had actually taken Mary to witch meetings—called covens—which had affected her not at all while her nurse lived to protect her and keep her from seeing too much. But Gwynneth had died, and Mary, who was often alone in the great London house, had continued to frequent those gatherings; one night, persuaded by a young man whom she believed she loved, she had become more than merely an observer—she had become a participant, waking from a drugged sleep in the bed of the man she had trusted, with a memory of such evil she had wanted to die.

Somehow, she had managed to get home. Fortunately, her father, being in Paris at the time, had known nothing of her adventure; but four months later, when she had the miscarriage that nearly killed her, he knew. After that, they lived as strangers, for he had never spoken to her again— not even on his deathbed.

"And then your father came and gave her the courage to live again," Henry had told me.

"Why did she confide in you?" I had asked.

"She had moments of wondering whether or not she was the right person to guide you. She thought she was overshadowed by evil, still. One day, she told me her story. She thought I would turn from her as her father had, but I recognized the truth. Mary was incapable of telling a lie! I respected her for telling me."

"I wish I'd known!" I cried.

"What would you have said—what would you have thought, Ada? Would you have given her understanding?" he had asked sadly.

I longed to tell him that I would have, but we both would have known I was lying.

Señora Mendoza had made me feel no better, "Always, she tried to atone. . . . Always she wanted to help you— but you were so hard, you made her so unhappy. . . ."

I sobbed, and said, "I didn't know . . . I thought . . . but at least you helped her. How did you help her?"

"I took her to the House of Tears, and I brought her the forgiving spirit of her father. I brought her, too, the spirits of your father and her nurse. I told her she should not fear the Devil when she died, for she was good, very good—of that I was sure. They could not touch her, those wicked ones—nothing wicked could touch her. I am glad I could make her a little happy before she died."

"I am glad, too," I had told her. "I hope that she will forgive me. . . ."

As I wrote that line in my diary, I started to weep again. "Oh, Mary, Mary," I sobbed, my grief as painful as it had been the day she died.

"Ada . . ."

I looked up, startled. "I did not hear you come in," I faltered, brushing my hand over my eyes.

"Come, I wish you to see something. You have done enough writing, enough weeping, today, poor little one."

I arose and let Felipe take my hand. He led me up on deck. "There . . ." He pointed. "See all the seabirds. We are nearing Valparaiso."

I looked up at the white birds hovering over the tall masts of the brig. "Oh," I exclaimed, squinting against the sun, "there's an albatross. I hope no one shoots it." To my relief, no one did. It flew clumsily, freely away. I clung to my husband's arm. "Oh, Felipe . . . I hope . . . I wish . . ."

He did not ask for an interpretation of my hopes or wishes. He knew what I meant. He said gently, "I am sure —very sure that Mary knows you are bringing her home to lie beside your father, my darling." He kissed me and I clung to him.

"Felipe," I whispered in a half-sob, "will she—forgive me, do you think?"

He said, "You chastise yourself too cruelly, my Ada—I think Mary had never any blame for you."

If our first-born child is a girl, we will call her Mary. If he is a boy, he will be Felipe Maria—which is one of the thousand reasons I am so happy I am married to a Californian.

ASTROLOGY...FOR YOU!

Your Own Personal Computerized Horoscope

reveals...

- **What You Are All About**
- **Your Life Style**
- **Your Success Potential**
- **Your Future... Next 12-Months Forecast!**

The wisdom of Astrology has enlightened people all over the world for over 5,000 years. And... now more than ever. You can share in this knowledge through your own personal computerized horoscope. It tells you more about yourself.

10 Full Pages All About You